BIG MAN

a novel

JA A.JAHANNES

Library of Congress Control Number: 2011939739
CreateSpace, North Charleston, SC

ISBN-10: 0984030719
EAN-13: 9780984030712

Art for cover by Lavar Munroe: www.lavar-munroe.com

Woman in cover digital illustration is from a photograph by freelance artist and photographer Ana Maria Agüero Jahannes: www.hamaje.com

Woman subject in cover design is Sara Lucía Agüero Jahannes.

Digital consultant is Tkeban X. T. Jahannes

Turner Mayfield Publishing Company, LLC.
1618 Foxhall Road
Savannah, GA 31406

BIG
MAN

JA A. JAHANNES

It all began with Brooksie Davis.

CONTENTS

ACKNOWLEDGMENTS

With appreciation to my editor, Betty Darby.

Special thanks to

Lavar Munroe, Connie Buckins, and Sheila Sawyer.

- 1 -

SHORT PANTS

reached under the jacket, lifted the pants off the hanger, laid the coat on the bed. I started to put one leg in the pants. I looked down. I gasped.

The echo in my brain was me cussing like a banshee.

I sat on the bed, picked up the pants off the floor. I held them up beside my leg. I cussed again, then threw the pants on the floor.

It all started about a month ago with a call from BeeBee.

BeeBee Curtis's broad, gray-brown, oversized face and big canine smile came up with his name on my cell. I had a feeling. That feeling came from a voice in my head, deep in a tunnel, under water, trying to speak to me, but I couldn't hear it. It always made my spine tingle.

"Big Man," BeeBee said, "I need a favor."

"If I can." They call me "Big Man" like people call small dogs Bruno. I'm a 31-year-old, lean, 162 pound, 5' 11" ex-high school and college basketball playing brotha. Sometimes I put on a big mind, until something shakes my bigness.

"Need a suit for my cousin Zeke's funeral," said BeeBee.

"BeeBee, you too big to wear my suits."

"I got a suit. Same one I wear to everything. Jonathan doesn't have a suit."

Jonathan is BeeBee and Cynthia's 14-year-old son. He was a half a head shorter than me the last time I saw him, with that same face as his father, punctuated by the bulging dark eyes of his mother. BeeBee and Cynthia live in Brooklyn. I live in Manhattan. Though the three of us go back to school days in Savannah, we don't see each other much. In New York an occasional telephone call keeps a relationship going. We see each other every other Christmas when some of our Savannah folks in New York give a holiday party. Same as it was in Savannah; parties only come around Christmas. Last I'd seen Jonathan was two years ago when we met up at Lloyd's townhouse for New Year's Eve. Then, I only saw him briefly. He and a couple of guys he knew in the building made a quick exit to play video games.

Lloyd was the one of our group living large. Brotha had a real nice crib, some fine women, an air of success, a white car, a white sofa, white carpets and white, white teeth. Even had a white full-length fur coat. He was a tall, gym-workout-ripped Mandingo, with reddish-purple lips and thick, bushy, black-as-midnight eyebrows that curved upwards at the outer ends. His eyebrows mocked the eyeglasses he wore. He'd been the captain and star player on our high school basketball team. For all his showiness, though, Lloyd seemed to have good sense. He was raised by his super-proper grandma.

"Okay," I said. "I'll loan you a suit. How you gonna get it?"

"Could you....?" I could hear that feeling about to speak. "Could you drop it by, Big Man? Cynthia's sick. I'm working 'round the clock."

"I'm off tomorrow. That's not too late?"

"Nah, that's great man. Funeral's not 'til Saturday morning. Big Man, you know I got yo' back whenever you need me. Cynt will be here. She's home with a cold."

"Tell Cynthia expect me around one o'clock. Going to Macy's in the morning." Carrying the suit all morning would be a pain in the butt but I said I'd bring it.

The next day, I looked through my suits and decided to lend BeeBee the blue suit which was still in the cleaner's plastic. I put it in a garment bag. I took the train to Macy's. Macy's was jammed with people. One clerk said if she'd known there'd be so many customers she'd have stayed home. It was like crackheads gone wild.

I tried to call Cynthia to let her know that I'd be there soon. No answer.

There was no answer to three telephone calls in an hour and a half. I finally got some boxer shorts, and returned the scarf that itched and got my money back. I decided I'd go over to BeeBee's anyway. BeeBee said Cynthia was home sick. Maybe she was in bed or had gone down to the laundry room or something.

As I waded through icy, grimy slush in from the subway to BeeBee's apartment building, my mind wandered back to middle school in Savannah when BeeBee, Lloyd, Cynthia, some other children and I were playing hide and seek. It was Cynthia's turn to find us. We ran off in all directions. I hid behind Lloyd's grandma's shiny new white Chevrolet. I waited to be found. The wait got longer and longer. I smiled to myself. She's found everybody else, I chuckled. Then Lloyd came by. "You still hidin'?" he asked. "Yeah," I whispered. He said, "Cynthia's gone home. She went home with BeeBee following her." I asked, "They just went home?" I never played hide and seek again. Now, I was ducking behind buildings as the New York hawk was whipping icy chills through my thermal underwear on my way to BeeBee and Cynthia's apartment.

"B. and C. Curtis," read the dingy tape under the buzzer at 3C. I pushed the buzzer. A soft voice answered, "Who's it?" Cynthia's words always sounded like a first generation foreigner on drugs.

"It's me, Cynt, Big Man."

She rang me in.

Cynthia looked her usual self. Thin and phlegmatic, eyes popping out of a large, sad face. Her compressed oval-shaped figure had small breasts at the top, and protruding hips in the mid-section. I gave her the suit.

"Did you hear the phone ring?" I asked.

"Yeah. I don't answer the phone much," she said.

My brain did a quiet somersault. There was that feeling again. My spine tingled.

When you go to someone's place in New York, they'll offer you a drink but never anything to eat. Grocery shopping in New York City, toting it home, and cooking it is too much work; but they will offer you a drink. In Savannah, the first thing they'll ask is, "Like somthin' to drink?" and then they'll go down a list of what they have in the fridge – fried chicken, baked ham, macaroni and cheese, collard greens – and absolutely insist you gotta eat something. Cynthia did neither.

I made small talk with Cynthia. All their wedding pictures were in the same place as the last time I was there. Large pictures of Jonathan were everywhere like they were watching me.

Life in the city propels you forward like a rollercoaster ride. It's fast, furious, sometimes scary. Savannah moves like peach cobbler, slow, sweet and lazy-like. In New York City it seems you're moving faster than time.

A couple of weeks went by. I'd heard nothing from BeeBee or Cynthia. I missed my blue suit. Finally, I called BeeBee's. No answer. I called several times. No answer.

A few days later I called BeeBee's again. No answer.

A couple of weeks later I was to head up my first meeting of the volunteer counseling staff for the Boys Club. I learned my bullshitting game growing up in Savannah, and I know how you dress opens up opportunities for you. I needed my blue suit to speak for me before I opened my mouth.

I called BeeBee's around 7 a.m. Cynthia answered. She said "Hey, ha you doin'?"

"Fine," I replied, "You okay?"

She went quiet.

"BeeBee there?" I asked.

"BeeBee's at work."

"Okay, Cynthia, I'm calling about my suit."

"Didn't BeeBee talk to you about that suit?"

"No, I haven't talked to BeeBee." I resisted saying, "Y'all never answer your phone."

"I'mma tell BeeBee to call you,'kay?"

She hung up. In Savannah, bossy women who meddled in men's affairs end up without their men. BeeBee had borrowed the suit.

A few days went by. No call from BeeBee. I called again. Cynthia answered.

"BeeBee said tell you the suit's in the cleaners."

"Okay," I said."When is he going to get it out?"

"I'll tell BeeBee to call you,'kay?"

She hung up.

Two days later, on my way to work I was going down the stairs of the West 4th Street station, BeeBee was coming up the subway stairs.

"Hey Big Man, how are you?" He looked hulkingly strong, in his heavy-duty work clothes.

"BeeBee, I done called you twentyleven times 'bout my damn suit now."

"I haven't been able to get it to you. Got it out of the cleaners last week. I work all the time. It's rough, man."

"When can I get the suit?"

"It's hard with me working all the time and Cynthia sick for a long while now. She's trying to get back up on her feet."

"Look, I'm gonna come out there and pick up my suit. Tomorrow around 7 p.m. Anybody gon be home?"

"Yeah, Big Man. Cynthia'll be home. Gotta go."

I said."I'll be there." I went down the stairs.

I was on time. Cynthia buzzed me in. Her eyes drooped and there was a curl around the corner of her lips.

I took the suit from her, still in a cleaners' bag.

"You have my garment bag?" I asked.

"Don't know what I did wit it." She didn't move from the couch.

It was cold and damp out. When I got back to my apartment I made myself some tea. I took the cleaner's bag from my bedroom closet and pulled the plastic bag off the hanger.

I took out my suit. Pulled the pants from the hanger. Put my foot into a pant leg. I went crazy.

I dropped to my knees.

Reaching for my cell on the table, I could hardly see how to punch in BeeBee's telephone number.

BeeBee answered. "Yeah, Big Man, whatup?"

"You cut off my suit pants?" The pants, cut off by about 6 inches, were lying on the floor mocking me.

"They didn't fit Jonathan."

"They didn't fit Jonathan," I said.

"I know you'd a done the same for me," he said.

I hung up.

I put my hand to my chest, my heart raced.

I needed to talk to somebody. I called Lloyd.

"Hey, Big Man, what's up?" Lloyd asked.

I told him everything. Then I stopped.

There was silence on the other end.

"Lloyd, did you hear me?"

"Yeah, I heard. That stuff's funny man."

"Why am I not laughing?"

"'It's not laughing funny. It's I coulda-told-you funny."

"Whatda you mean?"

"You know BeeBee and Cynthia are crazy."

"No! I didn't know they're crazy."

"They crazy, man. Been crazy. You didn't see it until craziness jumped on you. When they first came up here, they stayed with me in my one-bedroom apartment for a while. One night, they locked me out of my own apartment 'til they finished doing the nasty."

Lloyd cleared his throat. When people from Savannah clear their throat that means they're gonna tell you something.

"Big Man, BeeBee works jobs all over and ain't never got no money. Cynthia's sick all the time. Why is that?" he asked.

"Why does BeeBee work so many jobs?"

"'Cause Cynthia's always sick. Prescriptions, doctor's bills. Her not bringing in any money. I don't know, but the handwriting was on the wall, you just refused to read it."

"Why's Cynthia always sick?"

"She just is. Some people always sick. Even when we were in school she liked being sick. It's somethin' she cultivates."

"You cultivate corn, for Chris-sake, not sickness."

"And why they don't ever answer the phone?" I asked.

"That's what she does," Lloyd said. "When she works, she's a switchboard operator."

"So she doesn't answer the phone at home? Oh, this is really making sense."

"Look, Big Man, don't act like you're the only one in the world something's happened to."

He said he had to go. He hung up.

The next time I saw Lloyd was at a party after the wedding of one of our classmates from Savannah. I was wearing a new blue suit, underneath my leather jacket and scarf. It had been really cold out and I needed a moment to warm up.

I saw BeeBee and Cynthia when they arrived. BeeBee had on a huge off-brown unevenly faded trench coat and Cynthia had on the woman's version of the same coat, like coats from an irregular warehouse. I saw the host shove the coats into a closet just inside the bedroom. The couple came into the living room like spooks from another time and they melted into the crowd.

A few minutes later I made my way to the john next to the bedroom closet. When I came out, I saw BeeBee and Cynthia's coats sticking out from the overstuffed closet like the last five pounds a fat woman who couldn't button her jeans after Christmas dinner. My eyes moved to the bureau nearby; I spied a big pair of red-handled scissors. I picked up the scissors, turning my back on the crowd in the outer rooms, grabbed a hold of the sleeves of the coats. *Snip, snip, clunch, clunch.* It was done. I turned and entered the living room, which was filling up with folks.

Lights seemed to come on around me, the music began making its way through the room to me.

Lloyd waved to me to come over to where he was. His white teeth lighting the way like directional lights at an airport. I hesitated, then moved in his direction. When the crowd opened up I saw BeeBee and Cynthia standing there, too.

As the crowd shifted again and closed up, I eased into the hallway of the apartment.

Nobody saw me exit. In a moment I was on the elevator. There was a tingling sensation up and down my spine. I had a feeling it was time to leave.

The heavy banging on the door shook my apartment. I looked across Angela's still, firm breasts to the clock by my bed. It was exactly 3:10 a. m. The banging rattled the apartment again. Angela, my ex, who had made her usual monthly visit to me around 2 a. m., turned over but did not open her eyes. She knew how to get what she wanted and then zone everything else out, like she had done with our ten-year marriage marriage. I was what she needed an hour ago, but now she wanted her sleep so she could be gorgeous anchoring her 7 a.m. news broadcast. I grabbed my pants off the chair, slipped into them and went to the door.

I looked through the peep hole, standing to the side as though whoever was on the other side could see me looking at them.

"Who is it?" asked Angela. She was awake and realizing now that there was someone else in the world besides her and her light coffee good looks.

"How in the hell do I know? Looks like…"

"It's the police," she said.

The peep hole fish-eyed a man in a police uniform.

"Who is it?" I asked

"Is this the residence of Gary Johnson?" the man asked. "This is the police. We want to talk with him."

In New York, I am cautious even if the person on the other side of my door says "It's Jesus."

Angela was behind me by now, wrapped in my purple sheet. I could hear her breathing on my back.

"Open it," she said. She had a knowing intuition and a quiet authority in her voice.

I removed the deadbolt and opened the door.

Two police officers were there. The red-faced white one who stood a few feet back seemed to be the back-up man, while the oatmeal cookie faced partner was in charge of this episode.

"You Gary Johnson?" he asked. At the same time he showed me his police identification.

"Yes, what is this about?"

He read me my rights and then told me there was a warrant for my arrest, and I had to come down to the precinct with them.

I was in a holding cell, a small room with a nasty stained toilet, bars on the front, and three other characters who made faces at me when I looked at them like I had invaded some private club.

The wait seemed eternal as I kept denying this was happening to me. In about two hours, an officer came to the cell, opened the door and called my name. I went with him.

When the judge called my name in the mahogany paneled courtroom, I stood up.

"Yes, sir, Your Honor." I was trying to follow the protocol I had seen on TV.

"Mr. Johnson, you are charged with stalking, destruction of private property, and carrying a concealed weapon."

I gasped. I almost looked around to see who he was talking to.

The judge paused, shuffled some papers like he was shuffling cards in a deck. "Since you have no priors, I'm going to let you go on your own recognizance. I will set your trial arraignment date for …….."

I didn't hear what he said, I was in disbelief and the bailiff had taken the papers from the judge and was ushering me through the back of the court to an administrative office.

When I got out of the courtroom building, I called my office and told my boss I was sick and wouldn't be in. My boss said I sounded sick. I had not heard how I sounded. I was too numb.

I stopped at a coffee shop near where I lived. I dreaded going back into my apartment at the moment like it would make me re-live the earlier part of the morning.

I didn't want to call Angela because this would be one more black mark on that score card she seemed to keep that made her want to get out of our marriage, which was fine with her by night but a little too poor on the dayside of things. Angela had actually told me she could do better on her own just before our divorce was finalized. Stupid me, I had thought I was a part of her "own."

At the arraignment, BeeBee and Cynthia looked like a couple of hardworking, upstanding blue collar folks who were the backbone of America. They had brought Jonathan, who looked like a normal sixteen-year-old. BeeBee and Cynthia looked away when I looked toward them like they were warding off the Devil. Jonathan looked directly at me like he knew a deviant when he saw one.

BeeBee and Cynthia testified that I called Cynthia repeatedly and went by their apartment when Cynthia was alone.

It was Lloyd's testimony that was the most gripping. He was dressed in a winter white wool, three piece suit, white shirt and subdued green-flecked tie, and dark green alligator shoes. His eyebrows accentuated the testimony, rising and falling on cue.

"He was going through some kind of emotional crisis. He complained about what people were doing to him." Lloyd was compelling.

When I took the stand, I thought I was going to crap on myself. Angela entered the back of the court just as I took the stand. Since they were not letting anyone in the court at that time, I thought she came as the press.

I told the judge what had happened from beginning to end. He kept shuffling papers as I spoke. He almost chuckled when I mentioned the red-handed scissor, the concealed weapon, which wasn't even mine. When I finished, he put all the papers down.

"I've heard enough," the judge said. "Mr. Johnson, you seem to be a responsible man, but you have gone overboard."

He was right, I'd gone overboard.

He continued. "I am going to drop all these charges provided you attend anger management sessions for four weeks. I'm also going to issue a restraining order so the two parties are kept apart. " He signed several sheets of paper and handed them to a clerk, who gave them to the bailiff. "I'm going to fine you $250 cost of court. Bailiff, take Mr. Johnson out."

I went to the anger management classes, four classes, each Friday evening from 7 to 9 a. m. getting quietly angrier at the core of my being each week.

I knew it was time to leave New York. But I didn't want to go back to Savannah. Savannah had followed me to New York.

So I moved to Tucson, Arizona. I didn't plan to ever go back to New York or Savannah.

A year later, I was driving down Grant Road. It was a bright, sunlit day. Tucson's flat terrain and clean air made it easy for me to see miles far off ahead of me to the mountains in the west. Suddenly, I had a dark premonition like I was about to crash. I looked in my rearview mirror; no car was close behind me. At the red light, I glanced toward the car two lanes over from me. My stomach leaped into my throat, then nerves shocks ran across my back and tightened like a vise around my brain.

BeeBee was driving, with Cynthia beside him, and Jonathan in the back seat.

-2-

CANDLE BOWLS

A ngela, whom I'd almost forgotten I was once married to, called one day and asked if I could pick her up at the Tucson airport.

At the baggage claim area, she had me drag four large, heavy bags off the carousel.

In my car, I asked, "Angela, what's going on?" I could see her breasts begin to heave as she looked away out of the car window.

"I quit my job," she said. "Got tired of the same old grind. Crime coverage, make-up, microphones."

I could see now she wasn't wearing any make-up. She was so gorgeous I could lick her face with my eyes from the driver's seat.

"I've decided to become a novelist. Remember, I always wanted to write. News reporting and anchoring were just substitutes."

"No, I don't remember." I said. "You are going to be a novelist in Tucson. In my house." I blurted it out.

"You still love me, don't you?"

I wanted to say, "Seems like I'm still married to you."

She said if I didn't mind she would stay with me a while, figuring out if she really can be a novelist and helping me out.

I hadn't remembered saying I needed help, but evidently her post-divorce, monthly pre-late late night visitations for sex back in New York qualified as "ready, able and available," as they say at the employment office. In her eyes, I needed her. In my eyes, I needed disengagement, and her visits had meant I could keep my life simple because I didn't have to go out hunting.

"There's more," she said.

Oh my God. I looked at her carefully. She hadn't gained any weight but a vain woman like Angela wouldn't gain any weight. She didn't look pregnant. She didn't look sick.

"I'll tell you later. It's just 'til I figure things out," she said. "To be perfectly honest…" she started.

"Yes?" I was waiting for a bombshell. My ex-wife was moving in on me with four large, heavy bags, no invitation, no warning, and there was something "more."

That was eight months ago.

I kept a long row of little scented candles in glass candle bowls, along with brass and copper bowls, and silver incense and candleholders on the fireplace ledge in the big, open room of the house I was renting in Tucson. I got the house cheap since it was on a corner at the end of a poor barrio. The fireplace looked real nice when I first started to put the candle bowls out – festive – and the burning candles lent fragrances to the big room. It was a nice, ranch house with three below-ground bedrooms and lots of open space upstairs. The owner had used it for a bed-and-breakfast until she couldn't rent it much because the neighborhood changed its complexion to brown.

I liked the fireplace because I had never had one before. We didn't have much cold weather in Savannah. I enjoy the mildly cold weather whenever I can. In Tucson it was never like in New York. In New York, there were revengeful, cold snow storms and super slippery ice patches that seemed Nature's way of getting even for the hot air blowing up from the street pipes and out of the sides of buildings. The cold seemed to want to punish the crush of large, rushing crowds of humanity. It had only snowed three times in the thirty years of my life in Savannah. Each time only about three snowflakes fell to the ground, but streets were completely empty. Folks just wouldn't go out "in the snow." Savannahians don't even go out in the rain. You can cancel any social event if it rains in Savannah. God forbid it rains on Sunday – everybody's just going to Hell because they are sure not going out to hear the Word.

Angela took to lighting the candles around the fireplace, and curling up with a book to read on a sofa right after she came out to Tucson, four months after I got here. Before she came, she'd call me each month early in the morning around 2 a.m. That went on for three months. We really didn't have much to say, mostly a lot of breathing over the phone and talking about nothing.

After eight months of being enjoyed but not attended to, the little candle bowls got cruddy, so I decided early one Saturday morning to wash them and brighten up the fireplace with some new scented candles I had bought cheap – at three for a dollar at the Dollar Store. I put the glass candle bowls in a big pot, the kind my momma used to cooks greens in, and brought the water to a boil. All the wax separated from the glass bowls. I fished the bowls out, and set them aside, proud of myself for having reclaimed the bowls. A successful operation in the making.

Angela had curled up a lot of nights on the sofa across from the fireplace after lighting the candles to read or to write, but she had never once replaced the candles. She was good at keeping the large backyard raked, though. There wasn't any grass, but there were overhanging trees, a planted natural garden of huge rocks, a desert cactus here and there, and paths of light brown stones. It was the stones she would rake and separate from the small tree twigs that dropped to the ground regularly. I liked to look out the window to see her raking the backyard and rearranging the plants and dry wood sculptures the owner left. Angela was a different person in the natural Tucson air, raking stones. Yet, sometimes I'd wonder was she some kind of scorpion or deadly entity in disguise, something more than I knew or that met the eye. In Savannah, there were so many places to hide, behind polite conversation that told lies or in pleasant smiles and beguiling poses. Women as beautiful and charming as Angela were a dime a dozen in Savannah, but that didn't make them any less deadly. In New York, among the slickest people in the world, a Savannah woman like Angela would have fooled a bank president out of the keys to the vault.

I knew how true this was a week after she arrived when she told me what was "more."

"Well, I got an advance on my novel," she said. She handed me a roll of hundreds. "To cover my part of the rent," she said.

That left me in a quandary. Was I being pimped, or being kept? What was free and what was not free? I was smart enough to know that what is given freely could be freely taken away. Yet, I didn't have the courage to ask Angela if she planned one day to say to me, "I want you to take me to the airport."

This Saturday morning's adventure in reclaiming the fireplace candle bowls left me trying to figure out what to do with the water in the pot, now full of wax. I didn't want to throw the water out into the backyard. The wax would congeal, and there would have been a mess all over the stone paths or between the rock sculptures and tree twigs. The backyard had become Angela's pride and joy. She flew her brother, Tommy, out from Savannah and hustled him to install a beautiful natural wood enclosure around the large ugly cement deck out back. She had Tommy refinish the deck cement floor in a gray paint. Quite a lot of work. After he left, she went to work on the floors in the house. She was reading less and less on the sofa, and writing more and more on her laptop. The more she worked at her laptop, the more she worked on the yard and the house, like one fueled the other. For a long time, she forgot about little chores like washing dishes and seemed to enjoy her backyard projects. I didn't mind the little house chores, they relieved my tension from days of counseling school kids, who too often were adult problems in the making. I knew it wouldn't be right to throw the pot of waxy water out there. I wouldn't have thought twice in Savannah in the neighborhood where Angela and I grew up, where we always threw stuff out the backdoor where it belonged.

What to do with the water? I couldn't pour it into the kitchen sink, it would make a mess. I couldn't put it in the side of the sink that had the garbage disposal, that would be a mess. The toilet wouldn't do either.

I turned again to the kitchen sink. I reasoned that when I pour cooking grease in the sink, and ran hot water, it flushed itself through. I'd run hot water, and pour this pot of hot waxy water down the non-garbage disposal side of the kitchen sink. I ran hot water, poured the stuff down the drain. Over. Finished. Shined up the newly reclaimed candle bowls, put the little cheap candles in them, and sat them back on the ledge of the fireplace.

That night, Angela was particularly amorous. She showered early, put on her special Madame Rochas perfume, the one from our New York. That told me serious romance was in the air. I was mentally and physically preparing to rise to the occasion. Then, there was a tingling up the back of my spine, and a voice way off whispering. I said I can't hear. Speak up or be quiet. I shrugged it off.

When I snuggled up naked to Angela's naked body, I was caressed by her sweet breath. I could feel a gentle moisture on her skin. I had a feeling beyond the physical sensations of the moment but they were too mysterious for me to fathom. All else was drowned out, no voice speaking in my head for the next forty-five minutes.

The next morning, I went into the kitchen to take my daily 83 mg aspirin that makes me think I won't have a heart attack all day no matter how many crazy things happen to me and how many people become obstacles in my path to perfect days. I ran myself a glass of water and left the water running in my lazy, devil-may-care way my daddy scolded me for doing as a kid.

"Boy, don't you know water costs? Don't waste that water running it like that."

Seemed to me, as a kid in the hood, I had too much to worry about - people starving in China, and who has to pay for water in America. I was glad to have gotten grown and left home. In my own house, I could whistle at the dinner table. I could run water in my sink for as long as I like, as carelessly as I like, though I had learned who pays for the water. Still, I never figured out why people were starving in China. They certainly shipped a lot of rice to America.

I went to get the aspirin on the other side of the kitchen. When I returned to the sink, I noticed that the water wasn't going down. Maybe the garbage disposal was clogged. I turned on the garbage disposal, and let it *whizz bump grind* for a while. The water still didn't go down. After some early morning reflection, I figured the candle wax had stopped up the sink. I hastened to try to remedy the situation before Angela got up. I still recall the time, the first year we were married, that I was driving with her in D. C. and told her I was going to take a shortcut to a friend's new house through Rock Creek Park. That shortcut should have taken fifteen minutes. We didn't get there for over an hour to her constant reminders, "Gary, you said this was the shortcut." Seems like that drive was a pivotal point in our marriage. As I kept going round and round, stubbornly, persistently refusing to just drive out of the parkway, I heard a voice saying, "It's over, now." Some time the voice in my head is merciless. It gives stark warnings, in few words. Though Angela was quiet at the end of that drive through Rock Creek Park, I could feel her mind turning in another direction away from me. When we were divorced, and still spending those early morning hours together, she would sometimes mention the time I got lost in Rock Creek Park. I'd say, "Yes, what about it?" She would always say, "Nothing, just remembering."

I tried heating another big pot of water and pouring it down the drain. No good. I tried running the hot water in the sink for about a half an hour. I tried heating the pipes of the sink, that S-shape loop. No good. I cut the water off, and tried removing the pipes. Still, no good. I needed the right tools for this. Around this time, I also discovered that the dishwasher backs up when turned on because the water can't flow out of the pipes. I was beginning to hate candle bowls.

Before Angela gets up, I decide to call my brother-in-law in Savannah. I never call on him unless it's the last resort because Angela thinks he can fix everything, which is simply not true. I can fix anything Tommy can fix; I just don't feel like thinking about fixing stuff.

Tommy says, "Call a plumber."

I said, "But didn't you use to do plumbing?"

"Used to do a lot of things. But, right now, I'm in Savannah, you're in Tucson. Call a plumber." He hung up.

It's Sunday morning. There are no plumbers working on Sunday morning anywhere, maybe except China where they need to be growing more rice so they can stop starving.

When I turn around, Angela is standing behind me.

"What's going on?" she asks. Her whole demeanor has changed since last night.

I told her what had happened like I was making a confession to a parent, hoping I would get cut some slack.

She came over to me and gave me a big kiss.

"Call a plumber," she said.

"But, it's Sunday," I said.

"I know a plumber who would come over on Sunday," she said.

Something made me not want to ask how she knew this plumber, but I couldn't help myself.

"How do you know this plumber?" I asked.

She said, "You do, too. Been meaning to tell you. Ran into BeeBee the other day driving down Grant Road. We flagged each other down, pulled over to a coffee shop, and talked for a few minutes. He, Cynthia and Jonathan have been here almost a year, I guess. Isn't that amazing? You know BeeBee is a plumber. A handyman, really. He gave me his card. Got it in my bag. Just forgot."

"I'll call a plumber in the morning. A certified plumber," I said. I wasn't about to let a madman like BeeBee, married to a monster like Cynthia and the father of a space alien son, into my house. After what they had put me through in New York, almost getting me locked up, I didn't want to breathe the same air they breathed.

"Suit yourself. I'll leave BeeBee's card on the kitchen counter. Big Man, I've got some news to share with you." Her eyes got real bright. I got a small knot tightening up in my stomach.

This was Sunday morning. Why did I feel like there were demons at bat?

"Okay, what's your news, Angela?" I'm thinking now, it's calculated to kill me. I'm feeling vulnerable. For some reason, I'm getting an erection.

Angela reached up, put her arms around me, and spoke in my ear.

"It's all because of you. I couldn't have done it alone."

Now, I'm thinking, I really messed up. This is something that's gonna take something out of me.

Her tongue played around my ear.

"I finished the novel," she said.

"You did? Last night?"

"No. Last week. My agent called last night."

She has an agent.

"He sold it to a publisher. The long and the short is, I also got the film rights. Looks like a cool million and a half. Going out to San Diego tomorrow to sign contracts. While I'm there, I'll look for a place. I always did like San Diego."

"Just like that, Angela?'

"Just like what?" she asked.

"Nothing," I said.

"Gary, is something wrong? I thought you'd be happy for me. I couldn't have done it without you. Your company. The peace and comfort of this place."

I wanted to say, "You used me, Angela." But I couldn't say that.

I said, "Congratulations. I'll call a plumber in the morning."

That night I slept on the sofa. There was no light or fragrances from candles around the fireplace.

I called the plumber the first thing in the morning. BeeBee's handyman service card was on the kitchen table.

Angela was already up, packed and waiting on a taxi at 7 a.m. She was gone when I got home from school.

The plumber I called came at 5 P.M. He looked at me like I was a madman when I told him what I'd done. He also said there was no way I could have fixed the sink, as he removed the long s-shaped wax from the pipes. He charged me $100.

I saved about $6 worth of candle bowls. You do the math. I always heard you get what you pay for. Now, I am thinking, you pay for how you think.

- 3 -

BOBBY

"**M**om, what should I ask her to do?"

"First, find out what she *can* do." When I need commonsense advice, I call my mom back in Savannah. I was hiring a housekeeper who was coming in the morning but I didn't know what chores to give her.

"Thanks, Mom." I always call Mom before 7 a.m., a habit I picked up from her. When I asked her why she called my two brothers, my sister and me so early in the morning, she had said, "Because I want your undivided attention." But, even at 7 a.m., I knew Mom was dressed, her hair done, her face softly made up. Even at her age, she was still a good-looking woman with light brown skin, and vain.

Bobby, the housekeeper I was trying out, came the next morning at 8 o'clock. She'd been recommended by a guy I worked with. I'd never hired a housekeeper before. Over the phone, we had negotiated her coming two days a week, preferably Tuesday and Saturday. I knew they were odd days but she said that was no problem.

She got busy right away. The house was caught up in a mild storm with her moving about assuredly. By noon, she had cleaned the kitchen, vacuumed the rooms, made up the beds, reorganized the kitchen cabinets, swept the back patio, cleaned the dust from the sideboards, brushed out spider webs, washed, dried, folded, and put the laundry away, and ten other tasks that I didn't even know needed doing. I felt like I was breaststroking through a daydream, watching her work.

When she came into the open room with sandwiches for me at lunch, she asked, "Is there anything else you want me to do today? I have a list of a lot of things that need to be done, but I want good cleaning supplies." I saw she had put my household cleaners on the kitchen counter, lined up as though they were about to march off to a firing squad.

"No. I can't think of anything else," I said. I was surprised at how much of a mess the house had been in. I was amazed at how much she had done. She wasn't even breathing hard.

Our deal was that I was going to pay her $50 a day, two days a week.

She said, "I'm going to have to leave now to pick up my grandchildren. Getting started today was on short notice. When I come back on Saturday, I'll stay until 5."

I really didn't want anyone around my house when I get home at 4 p.m. and she had done more than I would have ever thought to ask her to do, so I said, "Bobby, why don't you just come in the mornings, from 8 to 12. I'll still pay you the $50."

"That's fine with me. I'll pick up the household supplies when I go out shopping. I'll give you receipts. You can pay me back."

Bobby was an attractive 50-something-year old, with beautiful rich brown skin, sparkling eyes, white teeth and a go-to-church pleasant smile. She was medium built with a small waist, ample breasts and a firm and round Savannah backside. She was about 5' 4" but seeing her work, she seemed to get taller and taller and stronger and stronger.

"Mom, she cleaned the whole place in the morning. She cleans like you." My mother was known to visit her kids, strip to her bra and a pair of shorts, and clean our houses or apartments, and cook dinner before we even got up in the morning. She was notorious with Lysol, Pine Sol, Pledge, Johnson's Wax, and standing in the bathroom detoxing the bathtub wall tiles with a cloth and a bottle of bleach.

"Good. Now, just make sure she doesn't steal. Find out what church she goes to?"

"Why would I find out what church she goes to?" I asked.

"So you can go with her. I heard that heathen ex-wife of yours was out there visiting with you."

"Angela's not a heathen. How did you hear that?"

"This is Savannah, Big Man. We hear everything."

I don't know why Mom didn't like Angela. They were cut from the same Savannah mold, good-looking, independent, vain and sure they were right about everything.

In a couple of weeks, Bobby had the house looking like a new place. She left me nothing to do, so I took over the backyard, raking, cutting, arranging plants and rocks, just like Angela had done. In fact, I was better than Angela had been, and I found the yard work therapeutic. It wasn't likely to help me write a novel as Angela had done, but it did release tension and helped me relax.

Angela called early one morning, around 2 a.m.

"Hey, Big Man. Did I wake you?"

"No. I was just lying here waiting for your call."

"Really, Big Man, you were thinking of me?'

"As sure as giraffes can fly."

"Are you being nasty to me?"

"No, Angela, I'm waiting to go back to sleep."

"Well, what were you doing? You sound angry, Big Man. Are you angry?"

"No. I was sleeping. Things are peaceful here, Angela."

"Like what? What's peaceful? You got a new woman. I can tell it. C'mon, Big Man, you got a new woman."

"I got a housekeeper."

"You're having an affair with your housekeeper? What does she look like? How old is she?"

"She's beautiful. And, I don't know anything about her age."

"You are sleeping with the housekeeper. How delicious."

"I'm not sleeping with my housekeeper. Actually, I'm going back to sleep."

"What do you want, Gary?"

"What do you mean 'What do I want?'"

"That's why I had to get away from you."

"What do you mean?"

"You don't know what you want."

I pushed the *off* icon on my cell phone and watched the screen go white, then black out.

The next morning, Bobby brought a little puppy with her to work.

'What's up with the puppy?" I asked.

"It's for you," she said. "To keep you company."

"You think I need company? Everybody knows more about me than me."

"That could be true."

Bobby and I had become friends. She was pleasant and without little issues. She was fifteen years older than me, but if she hadn't been my housekeeper, with a very strong husband who adored her, things could have been different.

Before I knew it I was playing with the puppy.

"What are you going to do?" Bobby asked.

"Who said I'm keeping him?" I turned the puppy upside down to be sure it was a "him."

"He's housebroken," Bobby said.

I named the puppy "Rascal." He was a mixture of a Chow, Rottweiler and German Shepherd. He was black with reddish brown patches. His black face was highlighted by a brown mask.

I don't know why everyone was assuming that because I didn't call some woman's name every now and then, or didn't seem to have females all over my house, that I wasn't dating. Actually, I was seeing two women, who were just as happy as I was not to be together all the time. A fortuneteller in Atlantic City on the boardwalk, about six months after Angela and I divorced, told me one night that I'd get married again, and be married for a long time. Since I'd only paid $2 for the palm reading, I figured it wasn't worth much and dead wrong. I certainly didn't miss Angela.

The only thing I was missing was small things around the house - socks, underwear, ties, etc. I told my mother over the phone that I was becoming absentminded, losing little things around the house.

"She's starting to steal. I warned you."

"Bobby? Mom, that's crazy. Did you hear what I said was missing?"

"Ummhum. That's how they get started. She organizes things so she's in control, then she makes you think you misplaced little things."

My mother, for all her smarts, could make up weird stuff, and almost make you believe it.

"Does she have grandchildren?"

"Yes. She's got eight, I think." I said.

"And, what kind of stuff is missing? Next, the TV will be gone, and you'll think it was a break-in."

Rascal and I were getting along fine. He had a personality of his own, playful, snappy and snuggly. He would snuggle up beside my feet wherever I sat down. He was easy. Bobby watched the two of us together as though she had been a matchmaker. She wasn't finished with matchmaking, though.

One day I came home to find her still there. She had a young woman with her. I couldn't see anything but the young woman's behind when I came into the kitchen. She was down on her knees with her head in the cabinet under the sink.

"That's Veronica, Ronnie, my second oldest," Bobby said. She came in while Veronica's ample, firm butt was giving me a show. The young woman pulled out of the cabinet and turned to me.

"Hi. You must be Mr. Johnson." She didn't get up off the floor, but smiled like she belonged down there and was quite happy looking up.

"I decided to put roach spray, ant spray and rat killer all over. When I get started I don't like to stop," Bobby said. "I brought Ronnie over to help me. We're going to do the whole house."

"I've got roaches and rats?" I asked.

"No. You don't have tigers and lions either. 'Cause we get to them before they can get at you," Bobby said.

Her daughter was still down on the floor. She had the same good looks as her mom, and the same pretty face, and happy smile. But, somehow, the lights didn't seem to be on too bright when I looked her in the face.

"Glad to meet you, Ronnie. I'll get out of you guys' way. Where is Rascal?"

"I had to lock Rascal up in his cage in the back. He doesn't like it none, but it's safer if he stays away from the places where we are putting insecticides and rat killer pellets. Wouldn't do for him to get to these poisons." Bobby said.

Bobby brought Ronnie over several times. She always managed to leave her daughter alone with me for some time. I finally caught on. She was hoping to hook Ronnie and me up.

Bobby was quite enchanting. She made my house a real home. She flavored it with small things that worked to make my home life easy. Over time, she had brought sunlight into the house. Sunlight agreed with me and improved my mood. She added little splashes of color. I like purple and orange. I never told Bobby this, but over a period of time, there was more purple and orange here and there. I also liked the smell of eucalyptus. I never told Bobby that I liked the smell of eucalyptus, but the candles in the candle bowls changed and ended up being sandalwood and eucalyptus. These fragrances soothed me. Bobby replaced the candles without my ever telling her.

Bobby changed out some of the cactus plants in the back yard, and rearranged the rock sculptures.

It was my house and my yard, but Bobby had worked a spell on it, and I was now completely in harmony with it. For the first time in my adult life, I was at one with the space I occupied. I felt free, fresh, respected, protected.

"What church do you go to?" I asked Bobby one Saturday.

"Why, you going with me?" she asked.

"Might."

"Well, that would be great." She told me all about her church. She made it sound like Heaven.

Not long after, I started meeting her at her church. I liked the 8 o'clock service. That was in the freshness of the morning. Service was short and sweet. The pastor was an attractive woman. She looked at me carnivorously the first time I went.

"Nice to eat you." I thought that was what she had said. She had the look of a hungry hyena.

"Nice to meet you, as well. I enjoyed the message." The pastor was very bright and simplified her message. She did not try to hoop like the male preachers, but she was kind and personable. She was a good teacher. She was charismatic, too, and made you seem like the only person in the world when you were talking with her. I got to like coming to church. Bobby's husband, children, and grandchildren all acted like I was family. Family I didn't have to take home.

Eventually, I told my mother about going to church with Bobby.

"Is she stealing much, now?" my mother asked.

"She's not stealing anything, Mom." Actually, I was beginning to miss more and more. I was down to about four pair of boxers and three t-shirts.

"Big Man, you never listen to me. There are things missing in your house. Stuff doesn't just get up and disappear on its own, boy."

Bobby had given up on trying matching me up with Ronnie. She knew Ronnie wasn't my type but she had been successful with Rascal. She had to try. I discovered Ronnie had four children, each with different fathers. Her mother was probably looking for some stability for her, too. I didn't mind. I still had two women I was seeing. They were different than the ones I usually saw. Different in terms of personalities, but the two were the same type, almost interchangeable. Neither looked like Angela. I was diversifying, changing my formula. It used to be light mocha, now it was sweet, dark, dark chocolate. The Dark, Dark Chocolates were a revolutionary new adventure for me. They were anti-Angela.

Angela and I started dating in high school. I liked Angela's independence. When I couldn't be with her, I didn't have to worry about it; she always had something else to do with her time. She never made me feel guilty for not being able to spend time with her. I never felt obligated to make up the time, either. I played basketball in high school and college. Angela followed me from high school to college. My college basketball schedule was pretty grueling. Early practices in the mornings, and late in the evenings. Away games. Angela never complained. Some of my fellow basketball players had their girls on their backs all the time because they couldn't make time for them. Angela didn't mind. She was like my mother, her own person, and a strong personality. Angela made her own way, on her own time. I kinda got used to it.

The Dark, Dark Chocolates were independent women, too. But they were needy. They needed me to tell them how beautiful they are. They needed me to tell them how smart they are. They needed me to be genuinely interested in whatever they were interested in when I was with them. They were professional women. They compartmentalized their lives very well. When I was with them, I was on their schedule. When I was not with them, I practically didn't exist. Independent, but needy. My Loretta Divines. Definitely new for me. Angela was not needy. And she had balls of her own. In a way, I was afraid of Angela. I was also afraid she'd show up again and try to take over my life.

I had gotten involved in the church. Not as involved as Bobby, who seemed to be on every church committee and was also the church treasurer. The church, the fulfillment I found in my counseling job, Rascal, Bobby's super organizing of my house, and the Dark, Dark Chocolates, put me in a comfortable zone to enjoy life. No major ups and downs, just cruising. No Angela smack-down surprises.

The pastor called me a couple of times on my cell. I missed her calls. I knew she wasn't interested in me. That was fine with me. She hadn't left any messages. I didn't bother to call back. I assumed the calls were a part of her outreach ministry, just calling to say how good God is, how he's blessing me, and to let me know she'd be there if I needed her. All of which I thought was true so there was no need to call her back.

I noticed that Bobby was becoming more and more anxious. It was not that obvious, but she was such a master of control that when she missed half a beat, I noticed it.

"How is your love affair going with your housekeeper?" my mother asked.

Anything could come out of my mother's mouth, so I wasn't surprised. Either she called me or I called her once a week and we were pretty much in tune with one another. She did the same thing with my brothers and sister; we didn't need to call each other. She kept us updated on what was going on with each other.

"The love affair is over. We've settled into an adulterous relationship that is quite appealing." I sometimes tried to be as shocking as she was.

"That will end with a bang." My mother said.

My mother's favorite conversation was her church and her pastor. Now that I was going to church regularly, I could add a sentence or two when she recalled all the goings-on at her church.

"How's that church? I wouldn't have a woman pastor," she said.

"I can't understand that, Mom."

"I just know that women keep trouble going on. They too busy. They are the handmaidens of the Devil."

I couldn't resist. "Being a woman, you should know, Mom."

"Was that supposed to be smart? I don't think so. Of course, I know."

To add something to her usual discussions and lamentations about her church or some other prominent church in Savannah, I thought I'd tell her about the preacher calling me. Savannah, with a population of 135,000 people, has over 150 African- American churches. The city is caught up in religion. You can't be black, live in Savannah and not know what's going on at most of the well-known black churches. And, every church had a scandal or two that is ongoing.

"She did? Called you?" Mom seemed fascinated. "What does she look like? I hope she's not ugly. There's nothing worse than an ugly woman preacher."

"You sure are hard on the woman folks. No, she's not ugly."

"All I know is, if she called you twice and left no messages, and you didn't call her back, there is trouble. Trouble, mark my words. Got to go. It's your sister on the other line. I probably have to hold her hand about something."

The next Sunday morning, I overslept. I missed the 8 a.m. service. I was used to my church fix, so I decided to go to the regular 11 o'clock service. In the back of my mind, I made a note to speak to the pastor about her phone calls after service if she wasn't too busy talking to other members.

I sat in the middle pew on the right hand side of the church. Usually, I sat down front but my usual seat was taken at the regular service. The pastor preached a good sermon. It was about change. Something about shaking the dust off your feet, and moving on from the old places where you had been. I kept thinking of Angela. This was a sermon she needed to hear.

After the service, I stood up at the pew, waiting for the members who had gathered around the pastor to disperse so I could have a word with her. I felt a tap on my shoulder. I turned around. There stood BeeBee, Cynthia and Jonathan. I almost choked. It was like a night terror had returned. My head started swimming. The whole ordeal of them having me arrested and the courtroom, flashed through my brain. I was feeling faint, but I held on. My mouth got dry; my eyes went hazy.

"What are you doing here?" I asked.

"This is our church. We go here," BeeBee said.

I started to walk past him, but he stood in front of me blocking my exit from the pew.

"Big Man, we're sorry. We're mighty sorry. We put you through so much. Can you forgive us?" BeeBee said.

"We're saved now, Gary. We're different. We're sorry we hurt you. We were in a bad place," Cynthia said.

I couldn't believe Cynthia was speaking English. I could believe these demons had the audacity to be here in front of me saying they were sorry.

I felt my soul leave my body and hover somewhere above in the roof of the church. Time stood still. Then, I came back to myself.

"Excuse me." I headed out of the other side of the pew, into the aisle, and out of the side door to the church. I was shaken but trying to keep my legs from buckling under me.

I could hardly eat when I got home. I had to call one of the Dark, Dark Chocolates and cancel dinner at her place. I needed to rest. To regroup.

Tuesday Bobby didn't come to work. That was the first time she had ever not shown up. I thought maybe some family problem; she was always taking care of her children and their children. Maybe she wasn't feeling well, though that was hard to imagine of Bobby. But, I didn't have any urgency to call her. The house was immaculately clean. And, since she had taken over shopping for me, everything was well stocked.

I was watching the 6 o'clock news with Rascal lying across my shoe. My mind was not really on the news, which was humdrum in Tucson, nothing like the big scale bombshells in New York or Savannah's well-aired scandals. Suddenly, Bobby's picture came up on the screen. The woman reporter was talking about a local arrest, the word "Embezzlement" scrolled up to the top of the screen, and there was a picture of Bobby in handcuffs, being escorted to a police car by two policemen. It all went by so fast, it was hard for me to figure it out.

I switched to the other news channel but they had moved to the sports and weather.

I called Bobby's home from my landline. The phone was busy. I waited a few minutes and hit redial several times, but I was unable to get through.

I picked up my cell phone, scrolled down to the last call from the pastor, and hit the call icon.

"That's what I wanted to talk with you about. We had an audit going on. I knew she worked for you. Wanted to get you to have her put the money back before the audit ended. It's out of my hands now. The audit went to the Trustee Board."

It was all too much to take in, and Rascal was being a nuisance while I was trying to think. I took him back to his cage. He didn't want to get in. He was used to being free. When I put him in the cage, he put up a scuffle, which caused me to push the cage away from the wall. Behind the cage, which was lined with a big fur rug Bobby bought at Goodwill, there was a stash of items

Rascal had apparently claimed for his own – t-shirts, underwear, socks – lots of my unwashed clothes.

I called my mother.

"Told you she was stealing."

"No, you told me to 'see what she could do.' Anyway, she changed my life."

I hesitated then said. "Mom, BeeBee and Cynthia live out here, too."

"I know. They moved there a couple of months before you did. They came by the house Christmas when they were in Savannah. Wanted your cell number. The construction company BeeBee was working for in New York moved to Tucson, gave him a good job, he said. Cynthia, poor child, always suffered from allergies, even when she was a little girl. Tucson's air is good for her. I didn't give them your number."

"Mom, you know about all that misery they put me through in New York, getting me arrested and all."

"Yes. But, I remembered how y'all played together as kids in Savannah. The big city will make you crazy. Besides, that was grown folks business. They called me once from New York to say how sorry they were."

"Sorry. Why didn't you tell me?"

Mom cleared her throat.

"I don't have to tell you everything. Some things you find out on your own. Or, not at all."

"Mom. I'll call you back later, okay? I got a call coming in."

-4-

SCOOTER

"**I**'m listening," I said. There are some calls that catch you off guard. "I'll think about it." I could feel my palm sweating as I held my cell phone. A flood of memories rushed through my mind.

The front door bell rang. "I'll call you back," I said. Rascal jumped up from the kitchen floor beside where I was sitting like he was awakened by demons.

The front doorbell rang again. Rascal's barking echoed against the walls.

"Cool it, Rascal. Somebody's ringing the doorbell, not breaking in."

No one ever came to my front door. I forgot sometimes what it looked like until I'd come home from a different route, and see the dust over what had been the deep red glossy front door with its tarnished brass doorknockers. Anybody who knows me or lives in the neighborhood comes to the driveway gate on the side of the house.

When I opened the door, there was no one there. Rascal stuck his head out of the door, sniffed and growled.

I closed the door. I heard the bell beside the driveway gate of the backyard. I went through the house, out to the backyard. I could see the young man standing there with a huge green suitcase. His smile radiating from seventy feet away.

"Brandon." I walked across the yard to take the chain off the gate and let him in. Rascal was right behind me.

"Yessirrr," he said. Rascal sniffed him up but didn't bark or jump up on him.

"Well, welcome. Come on in." He was dragging the suitcase across the stone pathway in the backyard with some difficulty.

"Need some help?" I started to reach down to pick up the back of the suitcase.

"Nah. I got it." He heaved the suitcase up onto his shoulders and toted it to the veranda, and then put it down.

"You came by yourself?"

"No. They let me off in front, but after I rang the doorbell, I saw the front door wasn't used much. I came around to the side."

He followed me inside. Rascal followed us. His ears stood up like he wanted to hear what we were talking about.

"This is the main room. The kitchen is over there. The bedrooms are downstairs. Follow me. I'll show you where to put your suitcase." He followed me down the spiral wooden staircase with the suitcase going bump on each stair.

"Your room is the third door to the right. You can put your suitcase in there. There's a bathroom in the room. When you want, come on back upstairs, okay?" Rascal had followed him downstairs, walking briskly beside him.

When Pastor Gibbons spoke to me about the church's program for pairing young men without fathers at home with men who could set an example for them, I had said "Why not?" From the moment of that conversation, I became paternal. I hadn't given much thought previously to children. It was kind of understood when I was married to Angela that we'd get around to it someday. We just never did. Now, I felt headed on that course, to become a parent.

I'd seen Brandon at church. He presided at the Junior Usher Board Anniversary during the 8 o'clock service. He was articulate. A smile played around his mouth as he kept things moving orderly as though he was having a laugh inside. He was more prepared than the other youth on the program and didn't stutter, misread or mumble during the program. He acted bigger and more confident than one would expect of a runty fifteen-year-old. He would be staying two weeks with me, and he had arrived.

"You brought a big suitcase for two weeks." I remembered the two week-long camping trips I'd had in high school when I only took a backpack. Rascal came over to sit beside me, keeping an eye on the stranger, his ears standing up.

"The suitcase? That's not all clothes. I brought my Xbox 360."

"Xbox 360? What's that?" I asked.

"My hook-up for my sports and shooting games. Glad you have a HD TV in my room. Cool."

"You're into video games?" I asked.

"And you're not. I thought that when I saw you at church."

"Why did you think that?"

"Maybe the way you dress."

"Like what."

"Kinda well-fitted." He flipped out his iPhone and rapidly ran his fingers across it.

"What's special about the games you brought?'

"They're the best to play because they have great multiplayer options. Video games are a man's best friend. I can keep in touch with my boys. And, smack them around a bit."

"What do your friends call you, Brandon? You got a nickname?"

"My friends call me Scooter. You got a nickname?"

"My nickname is Big Man.'"

"Big Man? They tried to call me 'Little Man' when I was small, but I didn't answer so they stopped it. You don't look like a 'Big Man.' I guess I'm supposed to learn something from you."

"Like what?"

"Some profound lesson on life."

He sat down on the chair opposite me. He was dressed like this new generation. He had on Vans sneakers, designer jeans, his New York Yankees baseball cap was cocked sideways, and a Stussy shirt hung out of the bottom of his oversized Billionaire Boys Club sweatshirt. Sunglasses with gold frames were in the neck of his shirt.

Rascal went over to sit beside him. He ran his fingers through the fur on Rascal's neck. Rascal was won over. He was easy.

"It's about 2 o'clock. Let's get something to eat. You want to go to a restaurant? Seafood? Chinese? What do you have a taste for?"

"Pizza. Can you call out for pizza?" He rolled back his right shirt sleeve and looked at his fake gold watch. "At 3, I got a game with my boy JC."

"Where?"

"Here. I mean I gotta hook my Xbox up. And my webcam and we'll play live remote. Pizza in is fine with me."

"Okay. Anything special?"

"You gon pay, or I'm gon pay?"

"I'm gonna pay," I said.

"Anything special you want?" he asked.

"No."

"Then I'll call it in. My favorite pizza place. They got all my info." He flipped out his cell phone, and quickly typed something in, then closed it up. "Shouldn't be long. They're not even far from here. I gave them your address and an order for two, Big Size, with two large Cokes, extra spicy chicken wings. $18.26. They take credit cards or cash in this neighborhood."

He was getting ahead of me. I'd already thought through the two weeks.

"Well, we got two weeks. You know how this Paired Brothers Program is supposed to work?" I was going to explain what I had in mind, and ask him to tell me what he thought we might do together, too.

"Yep. You're supposed to be a role model for me so I won't end up pimping my little sisters, or cutting the gold wedding band off my paralytic, half-blind grandmother's finger to support a drug habit. You are supposed to inspire me to look towards a positive future so I won't end up just being some baby daddy all around Tucson. You're to keep me from being a gangbanger or petty punk thug burglarizing folk's homes in nice neighborhoods or boosting in the mall. You're to help me stay on the straight course so I don't end up being in and out of jail like the other punk thugs, or chasing slutty girls to procreate another generation of worthless, shiftless pathetic excuses for human life."

"Re-ally? And what are you supposed to do?"

"I'm supposed to let you play that role if it makes you feel good. That's only fair since it's your house, and I guess most of the time, it'll be your dime. But, it's gonna be hard because there're so many people I'm bombarded with everyday that are setting bad examples."

The cell call from less than 35 minutes ago popped back in my head. I thought I'd not be able to put it out of my mind, but Scooter had knocked it momentarily off my radar.

"Who's setting all these bad examples?" Rascal's ears went up in the air again.

"The people in the U. S. Congress, presidential candidates, fornicating, cheating on their wives. Having to go into rehab for drinking problems. The city mayors stealing and bribing. Celebrities shoplifting and being recycled back into society. Sports brothers robbing and raping people. Isn't Jesse Jackson a baby daddy? Who you gon look up to?"

The food arrived. Scooter took half of everything down to his room, and I didn't see him anymore that day. I could hear him though, laughing and talking, I suppose to his boys.

The pizza was good, and it was big. Rascal shared mine. I made a mental note to get the order information from Scooter so I could order it again. After I figured out Scooter wasn't coming back out of his room, I went to my room. Rascal followed me, went under my bed and snored. I let the TV watch me for a while as I tried to push the phone call out of my consciousness.

In the morning, my Mexican housekeeper, Marta, made breakfast for Scooter and me, though I doubted whether he'd be getting up. I knew teenagers sleep late on the weekends.

Marta had made a delicious breakfast, too, though everything she cooked had the flavor of tacos. Maybe the pans had taken on a taco taste because of all the Mexican cooking she was doing. She was as efficient as Bobby, my former housekeeper, but slower. Marta always made enough to eat to take something home to her two children. She said it and did it right before my eyes. She was a gentle, solemn soul. She did not show emotions much. But, when she laughed it was like a well flowing over. Every time she had a good laugh, she ended up in tears. Rascal always enjoyed her laugh. He kinda bark-laughed with her.

I'd seen Bobby once since she had been arrested for embezzlement. I ran into her at the grocery store. She'd changed some. She no longer had that bright glow that she'd had when she was my tornado of a housekeeper. Her face was grayer, and she was sullen.

"I tried to call you." I said to Bobby in the grocery store. "To see if there was anything I could do."

"I know," she said. "You're a kind man, Mr. Johnson."

"Bobby, call me Gary." I said.

I had not really expected her to come back to church after the charges. Her whole family disappeared from the church.

"It's different now, Mr. Johnson. I loved my church. I'd been at that church since I was two years old. My sister, Janie, and I sat next to each other in that church for fifty-one years. I was baptized in that church, married in that church; my father and mother were funeralized from that church. I'm sorry it has to be the way it is now."

"How's that?"

"You don't know? No, I guess you don't. You not much of a meddler. The grand jury threw my case out. The church just didn't understand my bookkeeping. I'd been keeping the churches financial records since I was twenty, when some of those trustees were in grade school. Anyway, I filed a lawsuit against them. I can't talk about it, but it's going well. I'm at another church now." She seemed worn out, her spirit broken.

It was Sunday morning and I was going to church. At 7:30, I started out of the back door. The door was unlocked. Rascal had been quiet. When I looked out, I saw Scooter coming in the gate, bare-chested in a pair of oversized shorts and sneakers. He looked like he had been jogging.

"You going to church?" he asked. "Wait up. Give me ten, I'll go with you."

In a little more than ten minutes, he was at the car. He took the chain off the gate so I could drive out. He shut the gate back, and hopped into the car. This is what it's like being a parent? Surprises.

My mom called the Tuesday morning of the first week Scooter was at the house.

"What's he like?" she asked.

"Mom, which of us children did you like best?"

"Why you want to ask a question in the middle of my question? I like each of you the best. In some things, I like you best for coming to visit. You let me do whatever I want, and don't hassle me. I like your brother Raymond best for laughing with; he's got a very good sense of humor and he will make me laugh hard even in the worst situations. Remember how he had us laughing all the way to the cemetery after Daddy's funeral, about how Daddy didn't like lying deacons, and every lying deacon in the church had managed to find their way on his funeral program? Teddy, I like best because he'll always be the baby, and I can baby him, even in front of his friends. Sheila, I like best 'cause she has a good thinking head on her shoulders, and I can trust her to beat the IRS at tax time, to handle my money in investments and at the casinos."

"I meant as children, growing up, who did you like best?"

"How you gonna like children best? They are all the same. Give them what they need, and pray that they grow up to be people you like. People you wouldn't mind having as next-door neighbors. I know, I have prayed me up enough good next-door neighbors over the years and God's been good. This boy you got there has got you doing some thinking."

"Yes. First, I thought how nice it'd be to be the father of a teenager."

"It's more work than the Lord should allow," she said.

"Then, I got to thinking what about all those other years. The growing-up years. I guess what I'm saying is, I think I'm ready to be a father. It's time. Past time."

"Well, it won't be with Angela. She's getting married. Some Hollywood big shot. I got an announcement. A magnet to stick on the refrigerator to remember to hold the date. You know I don't stick any magnets on my refrigerator."

For some reason, I wasn't surprised that Angela was getting married. One thing I could say about my ex-wife was that she always knew what she wanted. Now, I wanted a family. And, when I get an idea like that, I move on it. It's like my basketball. I go into training. I play to score, and I don't stop until I'm the MVP.

I took Scooter to every museum and historic place I could find out about in Tucson. It was an education for me, too. Everywhere we went, I asked, "How much of a budget do you have? How do you get your operating monies? How many blacks work here?" People brought out their black staff to meet us. It was like I was doing a survey to see if Tucson was fair to black people. And, I never failed to ask about black people's place in the history of Tucson.

"I get it," Scooter said.

"Get what?" I asked.

"Black people have done a lot, even though a lot of the times they have been kept out, okay?"

"Okay," I said. I think I like this kid.

When the education tours were over, and even I had gotten bored, Scooter found an old rusty basketball hoop in the ground under bushes in the alley just outside the high wooden fence in backyard. I was sitting on the veranda reading the newspaper when he brought it into the main yard. I watched him clean it off.

"Where should we put this?" he asked.

Was the word "we" a word of ownership, possession or empowerment? Who exactly was "we?"

"We" certainly could put up a basketball hoop in the stones and soft dirt of the yard. The hoop must have belonged somewhere in some other residency of the house. Just before I could say "there," Scooter said, "Up there." I could see the place where the hoop had once been connected to the house over the side of the cement veranda. A perfect place. It had been painted over more than a few times.

" I know what you're thinking," I said to Scooter. "Where am I gonna get a ball? Look on the closet floor in the middle bedroom downstairs."

He beamed like he had found a hundred dollar bill.

In no time, we were playing a game of one-on-one. Every time the ball left my hands, it made its way to the bottom of the net. Whether I had dribbled down the lane and finished with a finger roll, or done my signature drop step fade away, it seemed like the net and the basketball were making sweet, sweet love to each other. It felt good to be playing ball in my own backyard. Scooter missed every other shot, but before long he was almost keeping up. The only thing keeping him behind was his outside jumper, or shall I say the lack thereof. While most of his points were made by his powerful hop step that he did every time before forcefully finishing under the hoop, most of my shots were from a further distance. I trounced him with two-pointers. I won. I was tired, but I was loosening up.

"How do you do that?' Scooter asked. He was curious about my persistent accuracy with my jump shots.

"It's in the wrist," I said.

I showed him the wrist action that had made me MVP and Athlete of the Week, and a few other names in high school and college. He was a quick learner.

"You play rough," Scooter said.

"It's basketball, not dominoes. It's a rough game. You got to go hard," I said.

I could hear him outside late in the evening bouncing that ball, and, then, no sound as the ball went through the hoop, and then hitting cement.

Scooter seemed to be gaining respect for my skills. We played again the next day. Scooter was no push-over, but I beat him.

In the middle of my education of Scooter, the two Dark, Dark Chocolates that I had been dating found out about each other. Seems they were shopping and met up at the same perfume counter.

"I didn't know you gave the same Savannah trinkets to all your ladies," the MoonPie-faced Dark, Dark Chocolate said to me.

I had given both of them a coral bracelet from a Savannah specialty gift shop. I had ordered them online. I didn't have a good feeling about it when I was ordering them. I'm not too keen on ordering things online, but I'd seen them advertised in a flight magazine. They looked harmless enough in the magazine. How was I to know that Savannah bad juju dust was on them? They didn't bring me good luck. But that night the MoonPie-faced Dark Dark Chocolate told me how she had commented on this woman's bracelet, and told the woman how her boyfriend had given her one just like it. They had compared notes and my number was up.

Neither of the Dark, Dark Chocolates would have been candidates for mother of my children to come. They had compartmentalized their lives. I fitted in. Children wouldn't have fitted in. I knew they would be phasing me out, and each would phase in somebody else to carry out the same roles that I was currently fulfilling. They would do this until they died. They were a new breed.

The last two days of his visit, I spent almost every hour with Scooter. He had moved the Xbox 360 to the open room upstairs. We started out playing Call of Duty. After I got good at it and beat his butt a few times, we moved to Halo 3. I got beat down a bit. Then we moved to playing NBA 2k11, a basketball video game. He finally had landed on my court. It was addictive. I couldn't get enough. I was The Heat and he was The Lakers. The scores were skewed at first. 81-101, 110-96; 65-90, 102-127. Then they got to be 82-85, 86-93; 110-114, 96-91. I couldn't stop. Scooter had to take over ordering take-out. Pizza. Pizza. Chinese. Pizza. McDonald's. Seafood. Pizza. Rascal didn't care what we ordered. He ate everything. He and Scooter became buddies.

"You like video games, man," Scooter said.

"How do you know?" I laughed.

"It's the way you dress." We both laughed.

I had on Jordan CP3.IV's and my oversized university sweats I ordered online. A matching set I'd ordered for Scooter was in his room. And I had on my Baltimore Orioles baseball cap, turned cattycorner, my Ray-Ban sunglasses were sticking out of my shirt. I couldn't wait for UPS deliveries.

"You think it's the clothes?" I asked.

I already had some of the clothes in my closets. I changed how I wore them. I guess my swag was changing.

"I guess you're not as bad as I heard."

"What did you hear?"

"That you were self-righteous. Always trying to show how good you are. And self -centered. I ain't saying they were wrong. But, you okay."

"You think? Thanks." I said.

"When you get an Xbox, we can play anytime. I worked five jobs for mine. Not all at the same time, though it seemed like it sometime. I sold my old games on eBay as soon as the new ones came out. Made money on eBay. Sold other friends' programs and things for them. Man gotta do what a man gotta do to be on it."

When it was time for Scooter to leave that Saturday, I felt like I was losing a buddy, though he had said he was gonna get even for some of my scores by live remote beating me unmercifully. He called to get picked up. His big green suitcase sat ready. The suitcase was heavier because every time we went to the Sports stores I bought clothes for him and me. Most of my selections were guided by nods of the head from Scooter.

"My ride'll be here in five minutes." He said. Rascal was down on the floor, his ears droopy.

"Your mom picking you up?" I asked.

"My mom doesn't drive. Besides, she always has to stay with my brothers and sisters. And, there ain't no baby daddies. My daddy gets here when he can. We think soon he'll have his papers. He lives in Alamos, Mexico. I think Mr. Curtis is gonna get him a job with his construction company, too. He'll be set, then."

"Mr. Curtis?" I asked

"Yes. That's JC, my best friend's dad."

"BeeBee Curtis?"

"Yeah. He's cool. My dad's cool, too. He'll whip holy Hell out of you on some NBA 2K11. I played him a couple the first day I got here all day long. He's a Lakers fan, too. He's at an American friend's house in Alamos that's got the hook-up. He's been busy ever since though, hustling construction jobs to send us money and relocate here."

"Your dad's Mexican?

"He's Haitian."

"But if he's married to an American, that makes him an American."

"My mother won't marry him. She says she doesn't want to be Haitian or married. He says, she thinks he's too handsome, and all the ladies will be running after him. JC says once he's got a stable job in the U. S., she'll marry him. I don't care. I think people ought to do what they want to do."

"JC is Jonathan Curtis?" The light on his cell blinked red.

"They're out front. Mr. Curtis and JC."

"Ask Mr. Curtis to come in a minute. I'd like to speak with him."

"Okay. I did learn something."

"What do you mean?"

"About life, from being here. Too much carry-out will keep you going to the toilet."

I couldn't help but laugh.

"We had the same experience," I said. "And, I learned not to judge a little man, until I know what he can teach me."

BeeBee came through the front door. He was as big and hulking as ever. He seemed more relaxed than he had been when he lived in New York.

"Lloyd called me two weeks ago from Brooklyn," I said to BeeBee. "He was in financial trouble. Said you and Cynthia owed him some money, but he had not been able to get in touch with you. Needed $1,000."

"Been meaning to call Lloyd. We can't be much help right now, though. Just bought a house. Bread's thin."

"I sent him the money." I said.

Rascal got over being down about Scooter's leaving quickly. I set out on my new plan to become a father. Now, I needed a wife. To have my own version of a fifteen-year-old like Scooter, I'd better start soon. He'll need me to be fit enough to jog with him in the mornings, and sharp enough to play fast and furious video games. I couldn't wait for UPS to deliver my Xbox360, my Call of Duty, Halo 3, and NBA 2k11. It was time I made a move.

- 5 -

SANCTUARY

'd come home. I'd come to start a family.

"Welcome to the Savannah and Hilton Head International Airport," said the voice over the intercom. "Please remain seated until…." How many times had I heard that welcome?

"The Savannah and Hilton Head International Airport" sounds big. "International" is meant to impress, but it more likely brings a laugh to first-time visitors. The airport has only one terminal and the facade is a warm inviting, homey brick and cement.

After two years living in Tucson, and almost ten in New York, now I'd be on dirt that was unlike any place else in the known universe. I'd come to stop that line of questioning that usually followed when I was home in Savannah: "Big Man, how many children you got?" Folks asked about the number of children I had and didn't bother to ask if I was married. I always wanted to say I had baby mommas everywhere and it was hard for me to keep ducking child support, but I resisted.

Mom was all over me as soon as I pulled my bag through the sliding airport exit door.

"My God, I'm glad you're here." Her light brown complexion was framed by bobbed salt-and-pepper hair. Her petite, ever-youthful physique in the off-white sweat suit and white sneakers made her look urban angelic. She never aged. Suddenly, her calm serenity vanished and she burst into tears.

"Hey, hey. Whoa. I'm just coming home. I don't plan to liberate Savannah."

She sobbed.

"Mom, Mom," I tried to hold her but she pulled out of my arms. I turned her face back to me, and looked her in the eyes. "What is it?" I asked.

"Your brother, Raymond, was shot this morning," she said through her sobs.

"What? When? Why didn't you tell me?"

"I didn't want you to think about it all the way from Tucson," she said. "I could kill somebody."

"Where is he? Is he …" I could hardly bring myself to ask what I wanted to ask.

"He's at Candler Hospital. He's in a coma."

"Where was he shot?"

"On Jefferson Street," she said.

"I meant him. Where was he shot?"

"In the head. Straight through the side of his head. They had to remove…" She composed herself. "… part of his skull."

"God, Mom. Where's everybody? At the hospital?"

"Sheila's there. Haven't been able to find Teddy. It was a drive-by shooting. He was just sitting in his car. Police don't know anything."

My sister Sheila had probably sent Mom to keep her busy, to distract her, so her blood pressure wouldn't go sky high.

"I'll drive, Mom." I put my bag in the back seat of her BMW. The rest of my bags would be coming with the moving company that was bringing my household goods, and my dog, Rascal, from Tucson. "Tell me everything, Mom."

At the hospital, with the monitoring devices attached to him, and tubes in his nose for air, Raymond looked like he'd been abducted by aliens. His face was peaceful, like he was playing a trick on everyone, pretending to be out of it, waiting to see if anyone would figure out his act. Sheila, her straw blonde hair mocking the neutral look of everything else around and lighting up the room, was by his side. She quietly stood up to give me a hug, then resumed her vigil. She didn't speak. Speaking would've broken the spell she was weaving to hold Raymond in her love.

How quickly life turns around. An hour ago, I was on a jet thinking about finding my soul mate in Savannah, now I was in Savannah wishing I could turn the hours and days back.

Mom went over to Sheila and put her arm on her shoulder. The two of them were identical. One heartbeat came from the two of them, like twins in a mystery that keeps rebirthing itself generation after generation within the women of our family. Mom had looked the same with her mother, and my grandmother had looked the same in the company of her mother. An unexplainable unity.

My baby brother Teddy still couldn't be found. Sheila, Mom, and I talked on and off as we traded places keeping watch over Raymond. We talked softly so that our spirits were attuned to the time and the circumstance. We could hear each other breathing. Most of all, we could feel each other's presence with Raymond.

Raymond's wife had left him a year ago. We didn't speak about it. Just like the family never talked about the split between me and my ex-wife, Angela. When Angela and I broke up, it was the first time anybody in our family, the extended family, had ever been divorced. No one talked about it. Except my father, that is.

"You couldn't keep that woman." Dad said about two months before he passed.

"We just grew apart," I said.

"Corn grows apart. People get married. They stay married. That's why there are all these loose women, now."

I didn't understand how divorce and loose women related, but none of his children ever argued with him.

"No. You couldn't keep her. I knew that when you married her," That's all he ever said about it. He'd know what to do if he were here now. I had to be my dad. Teddy could never be found when he was needed.

A nurse came in to check Raymond's vital signs again early in the morning. There'd been nurses throughout the night, doing one thing or another, but I paid little attention to them. This nurse drew the curtains back. The daylight spilled into the place like an animal that had been locked out of its home. She moved quietly through her chores, as though not to disturb me. I watched her absently. As she was leaving, she turned and smiled at me.

"I'm Donna," she said.

"Gary," I said. This was connection. It broke the stream of anguish that flowed in me.

"I know," she said. "You're Angela's husband."

I wanted to protest, but then she was gone.

The morning turned into afternoon. I finally gave in to my mother's request that I take her BMW and drive home. The empty house was a blessing. I sat in my dad's chair and cried like a baby. I had come to start a new life and Raymond's coma was a darkness that overcame me, smothering me. I didn't know when I'd be able to get out of the darkness. Then, I stopped crying. It was the wrong time to think of me. I didn't want to be self-centered, self-righteous. It was about Mom, Raymond, Sheila, and what Dad would have expected of me. I fell asleep.

When I woke up, everything was dark. I turned the lights on. The red light was blinking on my cell phone. I had slept through calls. I scrolled through the calls. Angela had called twice.

Moving around the empty house I saw the pictures, plaques, my basketball trophies, Sheila's cross-country ribbons, all the same things were on the fireplace mantel and around the room. The living room never changed. It was immaculately clean, as were the other rooms I looked through. I was looking for something that I couldn't name. I was looking for the answer to why my brother was in a coma in Candler Hospital.

When I went back to the hospital, all of the family was there. They filled the ICU waiting area, and spilled over into the hallway. Some ducked in and out, probably going for a smoke outside the hospital. One by one, they came to greet me, and ask if it was true I was home for good.

I overheard the conversations. Speculations on what had happened. Why the police was so slow to find somebody who had shot a black man. The shooting was probably a case of mistaken identity. Who would want to shoot Raymond? Raymond would be okay. Raymond was tough, they said. Sheila, who everyone looked up to, went through the crowd making everybody felt more at easy. Mom had just left for home. Sheila was leaving now. She looked tired. We hugged before she left. We'd always been close. I was the oldest, but she was only one year behind me.

The hospital watch went on for two days. Family came and went. Sheila and I were constantly with Mom, exchanging places. Raymond showed no change. The doctors didn't have any answers. They'd taken the bullet from his brain, but the prognosis was uncertain. All we could do was wait. Teddy still had not shown up.

"Where is Teddy?" I asked Sheila.

"Don't know. He disappears now and then, though. Usually he's with Raymond. I called his cell, no answer."

I spent hours sitting at Raymond's bedside. I was beginning to find sanctuary there, in that small room, closed off from the rest of the world. Raymond was somewhere else. Somewhere I couldn't go. But, I felt he was coming back. I talked to him in my mind.

"Remember how you used to follow me everywhere, Raymond? My girlfriends would say, 'Why don't you send your little brother home?' I couldn't do that. You were never really in the way. And, you beamed whenever I scored at the basketball games. I thought I could see it from across the court. I sometimes thought I was playing just for you. You enjoyed my success more than I did. Then, I was gone, and you were the Big Brother. Teddy followed you the same way you'd followed me. And Teddy kept you laughing. He had jokes."

"How are you, Big Man?" It was the nurse from the other day.

"Donna," she said.

"Right. Donna. You were wrong the other day. Let me set the record straight. I'm not married to Angela. Not anymore. We're divorced."

"Oh. That makes it different then." She smiled. I could see her dimples. She was very pretty. A hippy, full breasted Savannah woman, with skin like milk chocolate. Somewhere in the color register between Angela and Mom.

"That's better, then." She said. She had beautiful teeth and hair like brown silk. Her eyes were brown, big and wide open.

"You know me?" I asked.

"I was a year behind you in school. You played basketball with my brother and cousin. I never missed a game.

"Who's your brother?"

"Reggie Clark."

"RC? I remember you, now. You were always pretty. All dressed up, all the time. A proper young lady."

"Not all that proper. But I never missed a basketball game."

"Really?"

She was finishing her round.

"If you played, I was there."

I didn't know what to say. She took her clipboard, and closed the door behind her. The smile on my face would've made angels blush.

Raymond looked like a young Egyptian prince. Laid out, prepared to be the same for eternity. I left him, and went back into the waiting room. Only three of my cousins were in the mix of other families in the waiting area. I looked to the rear of the room. My mom was facing me, talking to a woman with her back to me. I walked over to them.

"Gary?"

"Angela?"

She stood up and gave me a hug.

"What are you doing here? I thought you were in San Diego."

"I've been here for three weeks. I tried to call you twice last night. We're filming the screenplay of my novel here."

"In Savannah?"

"The story takes place in Savannah, mostly. I came as soon as I heard. I've been up in Charleston for the last two days. We're also filming there."

"I'm going back in with Raymond," Mom said. She hugged Angela, let her hand caress mine and then left us.

"How long are you going to be here?" I asked Angela.

"I don't know now. I'm going in to see Raymond, too. I was here last night when I called you." She got up and followed Mom. Angela left me with a chill.

I saw my cousin Skip come into the waiting area. Tall, dark and serious looking, Skip went over to my other three cousins standing together near a wall in the corridor. He said something to them, and then they all looked at me.

"Big Man. I've got something to tell you I don't really want to tell you," Skip said. I stood up. "Sit down, Big Man."

As he spoke my body went numb. I couldn't breathe. I wanted to stand back up, but I was under water, and the water was not only suffocating but pressing down on me. I looked Skip in the face; I was trying to read beyond his words. My dad spoke to me from far, far off.

"Be strong, Gary. No matter what, be strong. Others will be weak, so you must be strong," Dad said.

I heard Dad in my head, but I was here, now. He was off somewhere. He was always off somewhere.

I woke up at home on the couch. Someone had put a blanket on me, but I felt like I was freezing. My mind wanted to retreat from what Skip had told me. To escape reality. I had come home to move forward, but all the pieces of forward kept getting thrown against a wall.

My mother came into the living room. She looked old, very old. The world had weighed her down, stolen her joy.

"Tell me it isn't true, Mom."

"It's true, Big Man. Sheila and I just left the morgue. God has taken so much from me. I can't even find the strength to argue with Him."

They found Teddy's body back in the alley where Raymond had been shot. The police hadn't done a good job of searching the area. Teddy had been trying to climb over the fence that separated the house on the street from the house behind it. He'd been shot six times in the back.

I took Mom in my arms and held her. I was here to hold her and to ease her pain. I wanted to get a gun. Dad kept a gun in his desk drawer. I wanted to go out and shoot somebody. But, Mom needed me here with her. Strong. Like Dad would have said.

I heard Sheila answer the house phone.

"No, Angela. We hadn't heard. Thank you for calling us. I'll tell Mom. You know about Teddy?"

"That was Angela?" I asked Sheila.

"Yes. Thank God for something."

"What is it?"

"Raymond is awake. Not talking but his eyes are open, and he knows what's going on."

"Angela told you?" I asked.

"Yes. She's still at the hospital." Sheila said. "Mom needs something to pull her back to life. I'll go in and tell her."

I headed back to the hospital in Mom's car. Sheila and Mom would be coming in Sheila's car.

Angela was in with Raymond when I went into the hospital room. She was holding Raymond's hand. I watched them for a moment from the doorway.

"Big Man," she said when she saw me standing there.

"Angela." I couldn't say anymore.

Donna came into the room.

"Glad to see Raymond is alert. How are you, Gary?"

"My brother Teddy is dead," I said.

"No. My God. Your poor mother." Donna said.

"Thank you. She's been through a lot."

"Is there anything I can do? Call me if there is." Donna wrote her cell number on her business card, and handed it to me.

"See you again, Angela." Donna left.

Raymond's eyes were moving though he hadn't said anything. He looked like he was taking everything in.

"I thought you were getting married in San Diego?" I said to Angela.

"No. I called that off."

"Oh."

"It wasn't gonna work. I probably knew that all along. Was just trying to get around it. I still wasn't over Raymond."

"Raymond?"

Just when I thought I'd been knocked down further than I thought I could go, I get plummeted into myself.

I was thankful that Raymond was improving. I was cursed that the moment's happiness was a pit where my anger couldn't find anchor. When I saw Sheila, I brought it up.

"I didn't want you to find out, Big Man, about Raymond and Angela." Sheila said. "I wanted it to all go away. Mom was really disturbed. Then, you said you were moving back home, and I had a feeling everything was going to crash in and it has. Sometimes things just happen, and it's not anybody's fault."

"Things happen that you make happen, Sheila," I said.

"Raymond and Angela have been seeing each other since you moved out to Tucson. I think they always liked each other, but never got together," Sheila said.

"Why did she come out to Tucson to stay with me?"

"I don't know. Mom was furious, but she didn't want to see you hurt. I could have killed Angela. I think she wanted to break it off with Raymond, but didn't know how."

"She used me."

"Maybe that was mutual."

"What do you mean by that?"

"Maybe you used her, too. You weren't married. She had as much right to be with you as you had to be with her."

"But, Raymond? My own brother?"

"She also had as much right to be with Raymond. After all, the two of you were divorced. Angela always loved Raymond. Even in school. He was too young, then. But not later."

"I didn't know that."

"You knew what you wanted to know. We all knew. Dad knew. Mom knew. We all knew except you." Sheila's words stung. She was not trying to hurt me. She added, "Sometimes you just don't pay attention, Big Man."

"Sheila, don't worry about me. I came home to start a new phase in my life. I'll make it happen. Angela may have outmaneuvered me sometimes, but I don't think that can happen again."

I sat with Raymond at the hospital every day. Mom had to make arrangements to bury Teddy. Sheila helped her, but had to go on with daily life with her own husband and children. Angela came twice to the hospital while I was there. Each time I quietly left until I thought she was gone. She was busy with the movie based on her novel.

I thought about Dad a lot during those hours with Raymond. If he'd been so sure of everything, why did Mom always seem to be in charge? Maybe Dad buried his head in the sand, or maybe he really was in charge, as I thought. It was hard to figure out.

Then one day, as sunlight shone in through the hospital room window, I heard Dad's voice.

"I'm sorry. I'm sorry for everything." It was Raymond. I could see tears streaming down his face. He looked at me. I smiled back at him.

"It's all right," I said. "I'm fine. Everything's fine."

He closed his eyes, and went off into that sleep where memories are locked forever and never return.

Mom was strong through it all. Two sons gone, and she still could stand. She still could speak. She revived. She glowed. Death could take nothing from her.

The police report said the informant told them the killers had been looking for "Pop." Pop was the drug lord in West Savannah. Pop was his street name. His real name was Raymond Johnson. His number two man, his brother, Teddy Johnson, was also killed in the Jefferson Street hit, the informant said.

Mom didn't read the newspapers after the first article. Sheila called the newspaper and cut off the paper's subscription to Mom's house.

The hardest part for me to imagine was that my two smiling, laughing, joking, even-tempered, raised-in-Gladys-Johnson's-house, saintly brothers were drug dealers killed execution style. Now they were gone from my life.

Two days later, I went into Dad's desk. Then, I went to the Spunking Club. I was on a mission. I got some information there. People knew me. Next, I went to Council's Lounge. The old familiars were there, and I got more of the information I wanted. Then, I went to BL's, the baddest club in Savannah. Anybody in BL's could kill you, and be smiling in church the next day. I got the last piece of information I needed. Bingo. I went to Dina's Restaurant. I sat at a table but when the fat man went back to the toilet, I followed him. I grabbed him in the stall, threw him down on the floor and dunked his head in the toilet. "You can try to get up, if you want to, but I wouldn't advise it," I said. I hit him several times with the handle of Dad's gun. It felt good. "I'm only gonna ask you one question, and if I get a really satisfying answer, I'm not gonna shoot you. Do you understand humor? Cause I'm gonna laugh if I shoot you," I said. I hit him again across the face, grabbed him by his neck and dunked his head in the toilet again. I stepped on his fat fingers, and shushed him to keep quiet. "Question. Who shot my brother, Pop, Raymond Johnson?" I asked.

"Antoine McGhee," he said. He was learning fast.

"Good. I know McGhee. Dack's Restaurant? I know that's two questions," I said.

"Yeah, Big Man," he said. I looked at my watch. It was midnight.

"There now?"

"Yeah, Big Man."

I stepped back, cupped his mouth and put the gun real close in his big right thigh to muffle the sound. I shot him.

"I lied about the one question," I said.

I went to Dack's. It was a half block away. Antoine McGhee was sitting at the bar, which only had two other haggard-looking fellows sitting at the other end. I walked up to him, pulled out Dad's gun. He saw my gun and held his hands up in the air. I shot him in both hands. I smashed his head against the bar till he passed out. The two drunks at the bar had turned away and kept drinking. At the phone booth on the corner, I called the police precinct.

"You can pick up Antoine McGhee at Dack's Restaurant. He killed Pop Johnson and his brother Teddy."

On the way home, I stopped by Laurel Grove Cemetery, jumped the fence, went over to Dad's grave. I dug a hole in the soft ground at the headstone. "Thanks for the gun, Dad," I said. I put the gun in the ground and put the flowers that lay at the headstone over the hole. I went home.

A few weeks after the funeral, my cousin Skip came by the house I had just bought in the Mayfair subdivision. He gave me a piece of news. It explained some things.

"Raymond financed Angela's movie pilot. He even paid for her move to San Diego. He was planning to move to San Diego, too," Skip said. "He thought he had outgrown Savannah. I told him nobody outgrows Savannah. Your brothers were good men. This is all they could aspire to in Savannah. They weren't lucky enough to escape like you."

"I always wanted more, Skip. I went away to find it. But, I wasn't afraid to come back and get it. I won't have any ghosts in my head. I'm still going to be the man I intended to be."

Skip said, "Like I said, you were always the lucky one."

So I was the lucky one. I guess the only way to break through darkness is not to be a victim of darkness. I'm glad I was here, to hold Mom up, and the family. To be strong like Dad always said.

"I'm the lucky one," I told Donna, on our first date.

"You are," she said. "So am I."

She took my hands in hers. "That's what I told my cousin, Lloyd, when he called from Brooklyn to see how you were holding up."

~ 6 ~

SEEING WHITE

Donna pulled up in front of my house on Pick Wick Drive in her bright yellow MG convertible with the top back, with rich brown leather interior. She looked like Georgia sunshine. Rascal jumped up and down at the sight of her. In less than two months, I knew she was the one for me. I'd had my eyes open since I'd returned to Savannah, and among all the pretty flowers, none were equal to her. I began to think I'd known her and been in love with her all my life.

It was all perfect. The invisible electronic fence around the front and the large backyard let Rascal, be free to romp and run, keeping him in while he kept everyone else out.

I asked the question that derailed my plans so innocently.

"How many children do you want to have?"

"I don't want to have any children," Donna said.

"You're joking, right?" I said.

"No." she said.

I played with my salad. I had to keep my emotions under control. The meal that she brought was ruined. Everything was ruined. I couldn't discuss it anymore, then.

I was still moody when I went shopping that evening for software for my Xbox360. I was going to install it when I got home, and hook up with my godson, Scooter, in Tucson and play him. I was glad that Scooter's mom had asked me to be his godfather before I left Tucson. It was a connection I wanted to maintain. Scooter was the sharpest fifteen-year-old brother I knew, and I was hoping that one day I'd have a son just like him.

"Would you like a bag?" the young African-American girl at the register asked me.

I leaned close to her over the counter.

"What did you think? I'm going to carry it in my hand? What are you trying to do, save the management bags?"

"No, sir," she said.

"Look, there was a time when black people couldn't go into stores. And, later, they could buy, but had to bring their own bags to the store. Their change was dropped on the counter. When I buy something, even if it's a ten-cent windshield wiper screw, I want a bag," I said.

She put my video game in a small plastic bag. I left the store. On the way home, I was still furious with the salesgirl for asking the question, and more furious with myself for acting the way I had. I don't think I made her understand my point, but I was in Savannah. I knew there was a lot about the world that wasn't understood in Savannah. I grew up here, but it took living away to make me realize that Savannah was a different world from the rest of America. Savannah escaped the trauma of the Civil Rights struggle in the South, and eased into a fake era of race relations built on deception from both sides. Savannah is racially schizophrenic. People say one thing in public, but in meetings, behind closed doors where real decisions are made, white folks make the decisions. I knew how difficult it would be to raise children in Savannah. I was willing to try but now, my woman had said she didn't want to have children. I kept thinking I should go back and apologize to the young salesgirl. How could she know the history of what my parents had been through? But, my parents had taught us. I knew if I went back and explained it to her, I wouldn't get it right. Might even make it worse. She was probably already thinking I was a butt-hole.

At my house, I settled into TV and a beer. The ringtone on my cell played a Scott Joplin rag. I looked at the name and pic that came up. Angela. In the middle of everything, my ex-wife, the devil in a pretty chocolate-brown face lashes would tune in to my misery.

"Yeah, Angela." I said. "No, you're not disturbing anything." That was a lie. "I'm doing fine. How about you?" I listened as she went on to tell me that the movie based on her novel had wrapped up. She said that they would be going into postproduction soon, and she was drained, exhausted.

"I got to go, Angela. Got to bring my dog in." I listened as she continued. "Yeah, I'll come." I could hear the surprise in her voice. I got the details. "I'll bring my girlfriend," I said. That was bold, I didn't even know if I had a girlfriend. Rather, I didn't know if I wanted to have the girlfriend I had.

Sunday, I slid into the pew beside Donna. I thought I was controlling my emotions since our conversation about her not wanting children, but they rose to the surface as soon as my arm touched her soft shoulder.

The choir sang like the end of the world was at hand. They were out of tune and pitchy, but they held their notes real long. Their faces were scrunched up like they were in pain. That was the winning formula. The congregation went wild. Some older sisters in the congregation were on their feet, singing louder than the choir, but the choir soon soared over them. The louder the choir got, the more people stood up. Some began to do a holy shout dance. The preacher stood up. He seemed ready to ride the Holy Ghost. With his brocade sash enwrapping his waist, looking like a Cardinal, he took the vocal lead of the song from the choir. He could sing. He knew he could sing. He didn't let go until the sho"nuff Holy Ghost Fire was upon the congregation. He really preached, then. The congregation was entranced.

Donna and I sat still. We were of the new generation, observers more than participants, analyzing rather than digesting.

I wondered if the pastor had a word for my situation. A word for Donna and me. I looked at Donna through the corner of my eye. She looked like the same woman I was in love with yesterday morning. How was I going to get her to change her mind about having children?

After church, we went to Jimmy's Buffet. She pulled her car up beside me in the parking lot a second or two after I did. She smiled when she got out of the car. In her simply cut blue-green Sunday dress, with her shoulders and neckline bare, she looked like a commercial for healthy living. She looked like the future mother of my children. I realized I loved Donna in a way I never loved Angela. Angela was gorgeous, exciting. I didn't regret being married to her. Donna was beautiful, gentle, easy.

Jimmy's Buffet was packed. The church crowd from many churches in Savannah was there as usual. Looking around, I could see various pastors, in their loud colored pimp suits and Broughton Street hood shoes, with their entourages, each a little wannabe Jesus out to fill their stomachs with chicken and Southern soul choices from the big buffet. Most of the pastors or bishops were surrounded by overweight members of their churches for whom Jimmy's Buffet was home every Sunday. There were more bishops in Savannah storefront churches than in the Vatican in Rome. Most of the sisters were dressed in poorly cut, oversized white dresses, trying to hold in their ample breasts and behinds. They were a stark contrast to Donna's simply svelte elegance and refined movements.

I ate catfish and lots of carbohydrates. Donna made a salad from the salad bar that looked like a healthy eating commercial on TV. We both had the iced tea. In Savannah, iced tea is the king of drinks at every restaurant, and has enough sugar to send a diabetic into the void between Earth and other celestial bodies.

I guess I was always one for going in when not expected. When we had settled into the lunch, and the place was calming down as food began to slow the mouths and metabolism of Jimmy's patrons, I looked Donna directly in the eye, smiled, and went to the heart of my dilemma.

"Why don't you want to have children?" I asked.

She got up without saying a word and went back to the buffet tables. I was left sitting there with the smile on my face trying to play off her departure. Was she being rude? Did she hear me? She must have heard me. We were sitting three feet apart. I was still smiling when she sat back down. With no prologue, she answered my question.

"Because I don't," she said.

"Where does that leave me?" I was still smiling.

All the way home I kept repeating her answer in my head. This wasn't getting any easier. Donna and I had been so right for each other until I asked her about children. Could I sacrifice wanting to have children for wanting Donna?

I heard the doorbell from back in my study. Rascal barked in the backyard. At first, I thought maybe it was Donna. She's coming to change everything. But Rascal's bark said to me, it's not somebody he knows. Rascal was a good announcer. He'd let me know if someone was coming, no matter who. He was also a good greeter. He'd bark hello to folks he knew. And, he was a good watchdog. He'd signal by his bark that a stranger was coming.

"Well, I'll be damned. Good to see you, Big Man."

Lloyd stood at the entrance to my house like a towering Mandingo obelisk. His white, white teeth greeted me. His thick, bushy, black-as-midnight eyebrows and reddish-purple lips were the same as always. His biceps bulged in his tight T-shirt. I could see his white Cadillac convertible parked at my front yard.

"Lloyd," I said.

"None other," he said. He gave me an old school embrace like we were still friends. We'd known each other since first grade but that was in another life.

I didn't back into the house to invite him in. I'd made a rule not to let anyone cross my doorstep that I had not invited.

"What are you doing here? How did you know where I lived?" I stood between the screen door and the beveled glass front door.

"My cousin told me where you live." He looked slightly uncomfortable standing tentatively outside the house.

"Who's your cousin?" I asked.

"What do you mean? Donna's my cousin."

Sometimes I forget relationships. When I left Savannah for college, I kind of forgot a lot of relationships I'd had growing up. Then I married Angela. Though Angela was also from Savannah, she didn't hold onto Savannah memories when we lived in New York. Donna had told me she remembered me from growing up. She had watched me playing basketball in high school. Her brother played on the team, and Lloyd, her cousin, had been team captain.

He stood there looking at me. I looked back at him. It was an awkward moment. It seemed a stretch of eternity between estranged childhood friends. I stepped back and let him in. Lloyd did three things that made a difference, one more so than the other two. The first thing Lloyd did was give me back the thousand dollars I'd given him when he had a financial problem. That opened up one door that had been closed. When I give people money and they don't give it back, or even make an attempt to give it back, I close a door on them.

"It was bad investing," Lloyd said. "I'm back in the market good now. Been meaning to get this money back to you for some time, but Big Man, you move around a lot."

The next thing Lloyd did was make an apology for the trouble he got me into when I lived in New York. He'd testified at my court arraignment that it was possible I had been stalking our schoolmate, Cynthia. He was the one who'd told me Cynthia was crazy, but at the trial he made it seem I was off.

Lloyd said, "I didn't mean to get involved with that business in New York with you and BeeBee and Cynthia. I know Cynthia and BeeBee aren't wrapped too tight, but you did keep calling Cynthia. That revenge you took on BeeBee and Cynthia, cutting off their coat sleeves, nearly put them in mental institutions. It wasn't right, Big Man. But, the questions I was asked on the stand made my answers get distorted. I knew what'd happened, but the answers all came out wrong. Big Man, can you forgive me?"

I told him I had forgiven him a long time ago. Otherwise that courtroom nightmare would've kept playing in my head.

I offered him a beer. We sat like old times, when we were in high school having a beer at his folk's home when no one was there. After the second beer, I asked him about Donna.

"Lloyd, I've got a real thing for Donna. Seriously. We've been getting along great. Great romance. Great companionship. The other day I asked her about having kids. She said she didn't want to. That floored the hell out of me."

Lloyd took another swig of his beer.

"Maybe, that was because of what happened to her."

"What happened to her?" I asked.

"She was raped."

"When?"

"When she was sixteen, I think."

"What happened? Who did it?" I asked.

"She was coming home from school. They never caught the man who did it. She couldn't remember anything except she was walking home from school. She never remembered anything about it. For a long time she didn't speak much. She was in counseling for awhile, which her father said was a waste of time. That fool blamed her. Said it was because she didn't wear enough clothes. He's a moron. She was never able to tell anybody what happened. Only in the last five or six years has she been social. That could have something to do with her not wanting to have children. I was really glad when she got involved with you. She called me in New York and told me the two of you were seeing each other."

Maybe Lloyd's disclosure about Donna's rape answered everything. Maybe, the rape left scars on her. Maybe she didn't want to have a family with a daughter who would be open to the same brutal, destructive act. Maybe she didn't know why she didn't want to have children. I was determined to be patient. I was determined to let her know I understood, I'd be there as we got through whatever had made her not want to have children. But, I still couldn't get over her answer at the restaurant, when I'd asked Donna why she didn't want children.

"Where does that leave me?" I had asked.

"What's children got to do with you and me?" she'd said.

"I thought we were headed in that direction," I said.

"Big Man, are you on some kind of mission? I was fine, just the way we are."

What had she meant? Was I overlooking something?

According to Lloyd, she'd received marriage proposals and had brushed them off and let the guys go. I forgave Lloyd even more after his visit. He'd helped me get a handle on Donna and me. I was going to give Donna all the support she needed to see that I was a man who could love her, and be trusted to comfort her.

At the reception to which Angela had invited me at the Hyatt Regency hotel, I watched Donna move through the room with ease. Her smile was as soft as cotton candy. She walked as though moving through a dream.

"You can't have her," A familiar voice behind me spoke into my ear.

"And why not? I already do," I answered.

Angela came around me to face me.

"You only think you do. Nobody can have her. But you would try. I know you, remember?"

"You know a bit about me. Because I let you. But I never trusted you, Angela. Yes, I'm saying this to your face, now. You know why? Look, there she goes."

Donna was talking with three young men who looked like movie stars.

"That a fact? I think I trained you." Angela said.

I said, "Yeah. I trained my dog, Rascal. And, you know what, Angela? He's house broken. Can't say that for everyone."

"Why did you come, Big Man?"

"Because you asked me."

"Wrong answer," she said. "You wanted to show me you didn't need me. But if I snapped my fingers, you'd be right back whenever I want," Angela smiled. Just as I was about to tell her what I really thought of her, Donna took my arm.

"Hi, Angela. What devilment are you up to now?" Donna asked.

"You know me, Donna. Always trying to keep my hand in," Angela said.

"Yeah, I know you, Angela." Donna said.

I imagined two volcanoes in quiet beauty.

"Let me get you ladies some champagne," I said. I walked away from them to the champagne bar in the center of the room. The narrow champagne bar was surrounded by people posing and posturing. All lower-level Hollywood types, I thought, but, then, what did I know about actors and acting?

When I rejoined Donna and Angela, with champagne in my hands, I heard Donna say, "You do that. You tell him."

"I won't have to," Angela said.

Before I could give Angela the champagne, she walked away.

"What was that about?" I asked Donna.

"About nothing," Donna said. "Can we go, now? I need fresh air."

I never thought I was afraid of women. I'd laugh when Mom beat me as a kid. It was funny to see the effort she spent to so little effect. But, I'm thinking now, Angela might be a woman I should have been afraid of.

I drove Donna to her apartment in silence. I didn't want to say anything. She looked straight ahead most of the way and occasionally she looked out of her window. I didn't want to be a part of any more negativity, so I said nothing.

"What do you think you were doing back there?" she asked. We had arrived at the front of her building.

"Hey, I wasn't doing anything. I don't know what you mean," I said.

She got out of the car with ease and walked away without another word.

When I think I have confused something and made someone unnecessarily unhappy, I try to make up for it. Been doing that since I was a child. On the way home, I stopped at the electronics store where I'd told the young salesgirl I needed a bag. I wanted to apologize to her and explain myself better. Inside, I went to the cash register where the salesgirl had checked me out. She wasn't there. There was a plump white lady with clown face red on her cheeks, cotton candy, gel spray bouffant, in a green plaid dress. I remember this because she was a sight that made me not forget her.

'Where is the young African-American woman who was on this cash register last week?" I asked.

"She quit," said the plump white lady.

"Quit?"

"Yes. Quit. This is America. People quit," she said.

"I'm sorry," I said.

"For what? Did you do something wrong?" she asked.

"No. But I wanted to explain something to her," I said.

"She's not here, and there is a customer behind you," she said.

I moved out of the way. On the drive home, I thought how life doesn't let us always fit all the pieces together.

At least, Rascal was glad to see me. I'd left him out in the yard. He was barking happily and wagging his tail when I got out of the car.

"What's up, boy?" I asked.

He ran quickly to the front door step, barked and wagged some more. When I got to the doorstep, I could see something bloody, red and furry. I couldn't make it out at first, but then I recognized its peculiar pinkish orange color. Rascal had caught and killed my neighbor's cat. He left the cat's body on the doorstep for the world to see his villainy.

"Rascal, go in the house. Go," I said.

Rascal didn't move. He looked at me like I was out of order. Was he looking for praise for killing the cat? I looked around me to see if any of the neighbors were out or looking through their windows, especially the couple across the street that owned this pinkish-orange cat. I think they called it "Miss Peaches." No one was about. I pulled Rascal in by his leather collar, and took him into the den and closed the door so he'd stay put. I got a garbage bag and put Miss Peaches' body in it, took it to the kitchen floor, and sat it on the tile floor so the blood would not seep out on my carpets. I went back to the front yard. Still, no one was about. I turned my front lawn hose on and started back to the front porch. Just then a car pulled into my cul de sac and proceeded slowly to my front yard. It was Angela. She got out of her car, locked it with her remote key, and started towards me. I started across the lawn to head her off from the front step.

"What are you doing here?" I asked.

"I came to apologize," she said.

I didn't want her to go to the front step.

"Don't know what you are apologizing for, but whatever it is, I accept. Now I've got some things I need to do, so I'd rather talk with you some other time," I said.

"Don't be like that," She said. She walked past me to the front step. "Aren't you gonna let me in? I don't want to stand here in the yard," she said.

"Angela," I said.

Before I could utter another sound, she had stepped over the blood and gone into my house.

I hosed down the step, making a strong spray with my fingers on the mouth of the hose. The blood dissolved quickly into the ground around the step.

Inside, I asked, "Angela, why are you here?"

"Don't try to act like you don't want me here," she said.

"I don't," I said.

"Yes, you do," she said. "You know it."

"You got me confused with somebody else," I said.

"No, I know you." She sat down in my living room like she was at home. "I've got something to tell you, and I want you to listen to me carefully. Donna's not good for you."

"I hardly think Donna is your business," I said.

"Everything to do with you is my business. I was married to you. 'Til death do us part, remember?"

"Well, you sure took care of that with the divorce hearing in New York," I said.

"I'd rather see you dead than another victim of Donna," she said.

"Okay, Angela. Cut the drama. What's on your mind? Then you've got to go." I said.

"Donna is my half sister. Daddy's love child. She has always hated me. She doesn't want you. She wants anything she thinks I have. She didn't want Raymond."

My brother, Raymond, God rest his soul, was he still caught up in mess? Savannah was like that. Mess followed you forever.

"She's using you to hurt me," Angela said.

I saw the lights of a car wash over my living room walls through the picture windows. I got up from my seat. It was Donna's car.

Angela saw the car pull up, too.

The door bell rang. Rascal barked. I stood by the closed door. Angela looked nonchalant. I opened the door.

"Donna?" I said.

She came in. Now, I could see the resemblance between her and Angela.

"What are you doing here, Angela?" Donna said.

"What I said I would do. You know, Donna, you should always take me at my word."

"And, you should always take me at mine," Donna said. Before I could register what was happening, Donna reached in her bag and took out a small pistol. She pointed it at Angela.

I moved toward Donna as quick as I could. I grabbed Donna's arm.

It was too late. Donna shot Angela in the left shoulder.

The police seemed to be everywhere. I wasn't much help. Donna was gone.

Angela said, "It was a strange woman. She looked crazy. She just came in the front door and shot me." Her arm wound was being bandaged by a medic.

"Is that the same thing you recall?" the police sergeant asked me for the second time. Angela had given her story three times now, and I almost believed it myself.

"Yes, officer. It was a strange woman."

"Can you explain the blood in the soil out front?" another policeman asked.

"I think my dog killed something," I said. Rascal whimpered in the den.

The ambulance took Angela to the hospital to treat her for her wound and trauma. I stayed at my house. Me and Rascal, alone. I wasn't thinking anything. Thinking had stopped for the day.

"Are you all right?" Mom asked. It was 7:45 in the morning. "Your sister said she saw it on the 7 a.m. news, and she tried to call you."

I hadn't heard the cell phone ring, but I'd left it in my living room all night. I wanted to resist the temptation to call Donna, and I had. I was putting everything on hold. I had decided to be self-centered and self-righteous. I was going to attend to me, and the hell with anybody that was going to get in the way of me finding peace with myself.

"I'm fine, Mom, a little shaky but I'll be all right."

"Of course, you will, Big Man. You're like your father, able to handle any situation. Besides, I need you to be all right. Big Man, I'm getting old. I need you."

"I'll be over tonight, Mom," I said.

That evening was one of the worst evenings of my life. When I was returning home from Mom's, I had a feeling that a change was about to come.

As I drove down the street that led to the cul de sac where my house was, I saw smoke in the air. As I got closer to my street, I could smell acid-like fumes.

I couldn't get to my house because the fire trucks and emergency vehicles were everywhere, blocking my street. I parked, and walked toward the house. As I turned the corner, I could see my house. Flames were shooting out of the back of the house. I was seeing white smoke up above the trees. The front of the house was a smothering blackened shell.

I panicked. Where was Rascal? He had been left closed in the den. When all had settled, Rascal was dead.

I moved back home with Mom. It was temporary, but it was a place of comfort.

I heard from Lloyd that Donna had checked herself into Savannah Area Hospital, the mental health facility.

"Give her my regards," I told Lloyd. I made no effort to see Donna, and I was determined to keep Angela out of my life.

Angela sat down in the pew beside me at church two Sundays later.

"She didn't want to have children because her mother has lupus. She didn't know if she'd ever have it, and pass it on to her children. Our father was a basket case; he had mental problems, too," Angela said.

I looked straight ahead for a moment. I didn't say anything. When I looked in her direction, she'd gone; walked out of the church.

~ 7 ~

WHAT LOOKS LIKE CRAZY

"I'm here to see Donna Nolan," I said. I'd no idea how Savannah Area Hospital operated so I tried to speak with authority.

A rabbit-faced clerk at the reception desk lifted her glasses. "Fill out this form. Been here before?"

"No. My first time." She lifted her glasses again, and twitched her nose.

"Let me check." I filled out the sign-in sheet. The clerk went to a small room behind the high sign-in desk, and began talking to someone on a phone. I'd ducked out of my office at school. I had an hour before I had to be back in my office for my third counseling appointment with the Inyang girl.

Donna, my girlfriend, had shot her half-sister, my ex-wife. I didn't know why. I didn't know they were even related before the shooting. I didn't even know if Donna would see me.

Savannah Area Hospital, a sprawling mental health complex of single story red brick buildings accented with white cement, looked like a community college from the outside. Inside, I saw a closed-in series of random assorted rooms and directions.

Visitors were being buzzed in and out of the locking color-coded doors to three areas of the facility by a security guard in a brown and tan uniform. I was feeling uneasy about locking doors. Ever since that time I'd been locked up overnight in a New York police precinct jail for retaliating on two unstable people, Cynthia and BeeBee Curtis, I've felt uncomfortable about doors being locked behind me. The New York incident had taught me I couldn't be sure about what looks like crazy.

The security guard at the desk took a piece of paper from the rabbit-faced receptionist. "You can go in now, Mr. Johnson." The security guard spoke in a low growl. She buzzed the door and another heavy set, moonfaced black woman met me inside.

"Follow me," said the moonfaced woman. We went to a set of doors. She opened the doors with a key from a large ring of keys. She beckoned me to enter. I felt cut off from the outside world as she locked the door and removed the key. I thought of my deceased father. We went to a second set of doors. The woman opened them. I entered behind her. I breathed more consciously. The air felt scarce as she removed the key from the door. I felt a sense of loss of control. I could see an apparition of my father walking with me. "Where are you going?" I asked my father. He said, "I'm here to show you how to act like a man." I said, "I am a man." The woman locked the doors behind us. My father laughed that shrill laugh of his. He said, "You should see yourself, shoulders all slumped." I straightened up my shoulders, held my head upright. "Leave me alone," I said. He said, "Okay, Big Man, remember when you went out for the high school Junior Varsity, you wouldn't listen to me about your jump shot? You didn't make the team the first year, right? You better go back through those doors and leave this woman alone." I conjured up Laurel Grove Cemetery where my father was buried.

The moonfaced Black woman led me through a third set of doors. She locked the doors behind us. My father stood mute on the other side of the third set of doors. He was saying something, but I couldn't hear anything coming out of his mouth. Beyond that third set of doors, Donna sat in a sparsely furnished waiting room wearing a green hospital-like top and stretch-waist pants.

"How are you?" I went forward to embrace her.

"Step back," said the woman who escorted me. I stepped back. I almost put my hands up over my head. "Didn't you read the briefing card in the lobby? No touching." I hadn't read anything.

"Sit over at the table," said the woman. She took a seat at the door.

"How are you, Donna?" I asked again. She was slow to speak.

"I'm fine," she said.

"Do you need anything?" I asked.

"No," she said.

I folded my hands in front of me. "How long are you gonna be here?"

"I don't know. I just got here. Yesterday. The day before."

She looked relaxed but her color was grayish. Her eyes had lost that clear liquid transparency. They were cloudy. She'd never looked frail before, but now she looked fragile. I wanted to hold her, to comfort her.

"Lloyd told me you were here. He didn't tell me anything else."

"Wasn't anything else he could tell you. I needed a rest." Donna said.

I didn't know what else to say.

"Are you going to the mall?" she asked.

The mall was nearby.

'No." I said.

"Oh, okay," she said. "I thought if you were going to the mall, you could get me some face and body lotion and bring them tomorrow."

"I can get whatever you need," I said.

I called Lloyd on my cell as soon as I left Savannah Area Hospital.

"Man, I went to see Donna. She doesn't look well. I don't know what to do. It was like we were looking at each other from the tops of distant mountains with a deep valley between us." I said.

Lloyd said, "She'll be all right. At least she'll be better. I'm just getting back to Brooklyn. It's a change from Savannah's oak trees and Spanish moss. Here, it's cement and cement."

"Tell me something. I don't know what's going on."

"Big Man, Donna's been in and out of Savannah Hospital a lot. She'll be okay."

"What am I gonna do. I don't know how to get her out of there. I don't want her there."

"You're not the reason she's there. Besides, she signed herself in. She can sign herself out whenever she wants," Lloyd said.

"Really. Nobody told me that." I said.

"You probably didn't ask. Where Donna is, people come because they want to come. To get a hold of themselves. Like I said, she signed herself in, she can sign herself out, when she feels she is ready," Lloyd said.

"What is she doing there?" I asked.

"Resting," he said.

"Resting? That's a spooky antiseptic place with people opening and locking doors like they're in Alice in Wonderland or The Wiz," I said.

"That's funny. About Alice in Wonderland or the Wiz" Lloyd said.

"Look, Lloyd, I've been in the counseling profession for a long time. That place isn't right. There is nothing about it that's right."

"That's right. Most of the people in there are there because right now they're a little bit crazy. But, when they're calm down like everybody else and get out, you might think they should've been in there. Some of us out here need to be in there."

"I don't like locked doors behind me," I said.

"Then stay your behind out here with the rest of us who aren't having a nervous breakdown. We're all the same. Depends on the day of the week, who flattened our tire, or took our parking space, or gave us a notice on the job. We are all crazy one day or another. Just pick the day."

"Lloyd, I have no idea what you're talking about," I said.

"Skip it. Look, Big Man, text me your mailing address when you get a chance. Want to send you an invitation," Lloyd said.

"To what?" I asked.

"To my bar mitzvah. No, to my wedding. Getting married next month. That's why I been running back and forth from Brooklyn to Savannah lately.

Was looking for a Savannah woman to marry, and have me some kids with. Tired of playing the clubs. Need a homebody to come home to. Big Man, you know me, when I go on a mission, I go on a mission. Came home three months ago, started looking around, scouting out the ladies. Came several more times. Not at the clubs, but at the Neighborhood Association Meetings, at the Economic Redevelopment Meetings, at the Jepson Center for the Arts. I wasn't looking for a Savannah Rat, I wanted a Savannah Praline, sweet, buttery and aromatic. I got her, too. I'm gonna put a ring on it, boy."

I didn't know whether to laugh, or to congratulate Lloyd. I thought he was so into himself, he couldn't love anybody else.

He added. "Sorry things didn't work out with you and Donna. Could've been good. Text me that address."

Back at school, I settled into my office. I had five minutes before meeting with a ninth grader, Samantha Inyang. After that, I was going to pick up the things Donna said she wanted, and drop them at the desk at Savannah Area Hospital. I read Samantha Inyang's file again.

Samantha knocked on the door. I asked her to come in and we started where we had left off previously.

"What do your friends call you? You got a nickname?" I asked Samantha.

She hesitated for a moment. "My family calls me Sammi, with an 'i,'" she said. "But, only at home."

"Can I call you Sammi?" I asked. She shrugged. Her hair was short, wiry and natural. Her skin was at the pubescent stage where it looked like liquid. She was short, petite, somewhat pretty and simply dressed in a loose-fitting cotton dress and jellied flip-flops.

"Sammi, I want to go over this situation again, to be sure I have everything, okay?" She nodded. She had been calm and patient throughout my questioning.

"Sammi, have you ever done anything like this before? Sticking a girl in the arm with a pencil looks very serious. The recommendation is that you be expelled, you understand?"

Her big eyes seemed to take in everything I was saying and look past me.

After my appointment with Sammi, I picked up the lotions from the store in the mall where Donna had said I could find them, and dropped them off at Savannah Area Hospital. The rabbit-faced clerk at the reception desk lifted her glasses as she took the store bag from me, examined the items with her glasses at eye level, filled out a form, and gave me the receipt out of the bag.

"I'll send them back to her," she said. She twitched her nose at me again as if to ask, "Is there anything else?"

I thought about Sammi all the way home. She had stuck a pencil in a white classmate's arm while they were in the cafeteria. The assistant principal in charge of discipline had written up that she had "stabbed" the girl. He recommended she be expelled. I wanted to counsel with her first. I'd seen her three times this week, and had kept the assistant principal's request for expulsion in limbo. What would make a ninth grader stab somebody with a pencil? There had to be a cause. Sammi was a straight-A student. Though she'd been at the school for a year, there was nothing else in her record but her grades, and this so-called stabbing incident. She didn't belong to any clubs or school organizations. I looked at her middle school files, too. She had almost a blank slate again. Her grades were excellent, no other activity or participation. Twice she had bitten classmates on the arms back in elementary school. She had started school in her native Nigeria. Her father and mother were English teachers at the university. Her mother was also a lawyer, according to the file.

It was hard getting used to being back at my mother's house after my house had burned down. Mom was always attentive, and it was good having the cooking that she made me love as a child, but I missed having my own space.

My sister, Sheila, visited at least twice a week.

"Mom, and each other, are all we have, Big Man," Sheila had said one evening as we both had wine.

"I would've thought we'd all be around 'til the end of time." We lost two brothers, Raymond and Teddy, to wanton violence, and Dad to a heart attack.

Sheila had her own family, her two perfect children and her perfect husband.

"Sheila, you're a Savannah Praline," I said.

"I am?" she asked.

"Yeah, sweet and flavorful," I said

Sheila said, "I thought you meant crunchy and a little nutty."

We both laughed.

"Lloyd said he is marrying a Savannah Praline," I said.

"I know the girl Lloyd is marrying," Sheila said. "She's more like a Marsh Rat. A curly-haired Marsh Rat that puts on more airs than Mon'que."

So Lloyd was marrying a Marsh Rat.

'You know her, too. Malaika Marshall," Sheila said. "She was in my Brownie Troop."

"She was the big girl with booty and braces?" I asked.

"That was a long time ago. Not so big now, no braces, still got back, though, kinda Janet Jackson back. In fact, she looks something like Janet Jackson, now," Sheila said.

"Lloyd's marrying a Mon'que acting Malaika Marsh Rat, a Brownie with Janet Jackson booty. That's his praline."

Sheila said. "I hope she's better off with him than she was with her last husband."

"She was married before?" I asked.

"Her last husband stabbed her thirteen times, that's what happened. On the front steps of their townhouse, and left her for dead." Sheila said.

"Wow. Does Lloyd know about that?" I asked.

"Don't know. He and you were living in New York when it happened. I don't know what she told him."

"Why did her husband do it? Wow. Was he on drugs or something?" I asked.

"Not that I know of. I asked her," Sheila said. "I spoke with her one day in the coffee shop at the mall. She said he had been really good to her when they were dating, and after they were first married. Then he began to be possessive. Wanted to know where she was every minute of the day. Checked her cell phone calls and texts. Upset if she even looked at another man. She became more and more afraid of him. She said when he stabbed her, he thought she was dead. Imagine his surprise in court when she came to testify against him."

"How did he get along with his mother?"

"That's what I asked. We both got that from Dad. He always said 'Don't trust a man that's not good to his mother.'"

"Yes. What did she say?"

"Malaika said he hated his mother. He wouldn't even let her invite his mother to their wedding."

"A man that hates his mother will kill his woman. They don't teach that in counseling," I said.

"Dad knew stuff that wasn't in the books."

"Yeah. I know. He told us enough," I said.

Mom came into the kitchen.

"Sheila, I fixed you some food. It's in the fridge. Some of it's in Tupperware, and some of it's in aluminum foil. It's all together on the kitchen counter."

She said, "Mom you didn't have to do that. I've already cooked at home."

"It wasn't any trouble. I fixed all the things you like. Enough for two meals. You can freeze the crab cakes, if the four of you don't eat them all at one time. What can I fix for you, Big Man? Got a ham I could make sandwiches from. Potato salad? Baked chicken?"

"Nothing, Mom. I just ate a hamburger and fries before I got home." I said.

Mom stared at me. The hair on the back of my neck stood up. Then she took a deep breath.

"I cook plenty of perfectly good food. It was good enough to make y'all healthy growing up. You go out and eat a hamburger made of worms, and potato fries that taste like sawdust. If I'd fed you that kind of poison growing up, you'd be brain dead. Do you know how many nitrates and other chemicals that's in that carryout food?"

"Mom, it was just a hamburger and a small bag of fries, not the whole of China," I said.

"That's where they should take that slop, to China. To get back for the soy soaked Chinese food that's poisoning America," Mom said.

Sheila said, "I got to go. Got to pick up the children from the mall. Late already."

"Take your food before you stop off at a fast-food killing house, and end up poisoning my grandchildren," Mom said.

Sheila got the food from the refrigerator, and Mom put it in a recycled plastic store bag. Sheila was off. I was left wanting to know more about Marsh Rat Malaika, and wondering if Lloyd knew what he was getting into.

Most of the time at Mom's house, I sat on the back closed-in sun porch and reviewed the files of my counselees at school or played video games with my godson, Scooter, in Tucson by Skype. Scooter had a girl now so his conversation was beginning to take a new road. He was sixteen, and ready for experimentation. He trusted me to be honest with him.

"So how do you know if a girl really, really likes you?" Scooter asked one evening at the end of a game. He was asking the wrong man. But, I couldn't tell him that. He looked up to me. I was supposed to answer questions with authority. The two women I thought had loved me, my ex-wife Angela, and her who-knew half-sister, Donna, had been mirages. The only ones that had been real were the Dark, Dark Chocolates I had dated in Tucson, but neither of them wanted to have a family. They both wanted freedom with arranged nights and occasional social outings with their man.

"You can tell if a woman really likes you if she doesn't get upset when she sees you with another woman," I said.

"Really," Scooter asked.

"Yeah," I said.

The week went by fast. I visited Donna twice. On the third visit, she was gone. She had checked herself out. The Savannah Area Hospital rabbit face woman said she could not tell me where an ex-patient had gone. It was policy. I called Donna's cell. I got that "If you feel you have reached this number in error, please hang up and try again" message.

It was Friday afternoon, and I had one more counseling appointment. It was with Mrs. Inyang, Samantha's mother.

From my office window, I could see Mrs. Inyang get out of her car in the Visitors Parking Lot and walk toward the front entrance of the school.

She was a thirtyish Nigerian woman, who walked like the crowns of Africa belonged to her, and the sunshine was blessed for shining on her. Her African dress wasn't those oversized mumus American sistas wear every Black History Month. Her outfit was elaborate, chic, cosmopolitan and stitched to fit her curvaceous body like skin, and it was topped off by an elaborate gele headwrap in matching midnight blue indigo fabric. Every time I'd seen her, she was so elegant, her walk and her demeanor so regal, that I thought of her for days afterward.

At the end of our meeting, I summarized what I thought to be the case for Mrs. Inyang with her daughter.

"She stuck that girl with the pencil because she was verbally abused, ostracized and traumatized until she didn't know any other way to retaliate."

"So what are we going to do?" Mrs. Inyang asked.

"I am going to counsel with Sammi," I said.

"Thank you," she said. She took my hands across the corner of my desk.

"I'm going to help her see the whole situation that she's been in since she came to the U.S." I said.

"We didn't have anything like this when she was in grade school in Nigeria. There, everybody loved Sammi. She was a good student, a happy, sweet girl," She let go of my hands.

"Yes. In Nigeria, she didn't have to carry three hundred years of slavery like a bull's-eye on her back. Sammi has been a target of racial slurs. Kids have called her names, jungle bunny, Buckwheat, Hottentot, Sambo girl. They've scorned her and verbally abused her. Not just the white kids, black kids too, and the girl she stabbed was a ringleader, though her folks are far less educated or sophisticated than you and your husband. The worst part is the teachers have never tried to stop the abuse."

"This is very sad, Mr. Johnson. We moved to the United States for a better life, not to throw our daughter into … Hell." Mrs. Inyang looked like she was on the verge of tears. I wanted to take her in my arms and comfort her.

"Mrs. Inyang, I am going to do everything I can. I'll also ask to have the girl that she stuck with the pencil expelled. That probably won't work. But, it will put them on equal footing. Might help if you ask for the same thing until the issue is resolved. I will meet with the teacher and the students in the class. I assure you, I will do my best to put an end to this. Most importantly, I'll work with Sammi so she can learn how to deal with ugliness in a protective way and win."

I could see moisture taking over Mrs. Inyang's eyes. Again I wanted to take her in my arms, but I resisted.

"Mr. Johnson, I appreciate you. You don't know how much. This is a bad time, anyway. My husband and I have just divorced. We are still friends, but he is going back to Nigeria soon and poor Sammi will have only me."

"Mrs. Inyang, I'll do my best. I'll keep you posted. Here's my card. I'll put my personal cell number on the back." I handed her one of the cards the school printed for counselors. "If you need anything, call me," I said.

That evening Donna texted me. Her message said, "I haven't changed my mind. I don't want to have children. I like you, but I'm not in love with you." I texted her back almost automatically, "Okay. Haven't changed my mind either. I want to have children." I could imagine my father having something to say about that but I wouldn't have listened to him. He didn't know crazy like I knew crazy.

Trying to get over the fire that had gutted my previous house and forced me to temporarily move back home with Mom, I found a house for myself in the Mayfair subdivision of Savannah, near Lake Mayer. It was a good location because it was surrounded by sports complexes, the county aquatic center, a soccer complex, tennis courts, two baseball fields, and not far from a world-class weightlifting facility. It was time to get my exercise on, and to exorcise the women demons that had been plaguing my life.

Mom and Sheila helped take care of my packing up and getting me ready to move in. My insurance company had been very helpful in getting me financially ready for the move. I knew I could never replace everything, but the fire that burned down my house might have been a way of ridding me of old troubles.

The next time I saw Donna was at Lloyd's wedding. She and her half-sister, my ex-wife, Angela were together. They were both beautiful. I saw them from across the sanctuary as I took my seat. I did not look directly at them, and they didn't seem to have any trouble avoiding looking in my direction. They were Savannah beauties. Beautiful poison.

My date had stopped at the entrance to the church to speak to some friends. When she came into the sanctuary to join me, I could see all eyes on her. I lifted my arm in the air so she could see me when she entered.

The sunlight shone brightly through the huge stained glass windows of the church as Deborah Inyang moved towards me looking like Miss Universe.

Malaika was radiant in her white wedding dress. Lloyd was handsome in his classic black, traditional tuxedo, and his thick, bushy, black-as-midnight eyebrows looking slicked down for the occasion. His cousin, JC, my old basketball playing high school classmate and the groom's cousin, was the best man. Cynthia Curtis, who with her husband, BeeBee, had once had me jailed in New York, was the maid of honor. I hadn't seen Cynthia since I'd left Tucson. She had changed. She was actually pretty and she looked healthy. BeeBee was in the crowd, too. We'd said our hellos on the way into the church. It was a real Savannah wedding. All the Savannah men were handsome, and all the Savannah women were beautiful. Deborah Inyang was more beautiful than all the rest.

I was happy. The sun was bright. The skies were clear. I wondered how long the good weather would last.

~ 8 ~

SUMMER HEAT

Deborah's dark brown eyes looked up at me across the breakfast table. I looked over her head. I'd been staring at her. When our eyes met again, her smile lit up the breakfast nook.

Her black skin against my oversized white T-shirt was smooth silk. The T-shirt draped low off her shoulders and fell upon the contours of her breasts.

"Thank you," she said.

"For what?" I asked.

"For last night."

"Hope I gave as good as I got."

"It was a good game of Scrabble. Don't often get to play with a jock." This time I smiled.

I felt like I'd been hit with sugar-good luck, like hitting the lottery. I couldn't come down from the high I'd been feeling as Deborah Inyang and I kept this dance of souls going day after day, touching and breathing each other in.

She got up from the table, taking her dishes and mine to the sink. I couldn't take my eyes off her. It had only been a short time since we began seeing each other, but it was like I'd been with her every day forever.

"Got to pick Sammi up. Her camp lets out at noon." She looked at her cell phone. "It's eleven now. Don't want to be one of those mothers who shows up late 'cause she can't pull herself away from her man. So I've got to get dressed," she said. Her voice echoed, "So I've got to get dressed. ….got to get dressed."

"Woman, you've bewitched me," I said. She let her fingers play across the back of my neck. She kissed me behind both ears. Everything she did sent me tingling.

I pulled her around to me, down into my arms and my tongue found hers.

She was leaving the bedroom at ten to twelve. I was drained. My mind was consumed with her. I heard the front door close. It was going to be a real lazy Saturday.

A sound like a car backfiring punctured my reverie. Then I heard it again. It wasn't a car, it was gunshots.

I went to the front window. A weird dream was descending on me. Deborah lay on the lawn in front of the house. There was an empty silence in the neighborhood. Nothing moved, not even the air.

I couldn't see. I reached my hands out to find something in the dark. I woke up. Cold sweat covered my forehead. In a ray of moonlight washing through the window, I saw Deborah on the pillow next to me in my baby blue pajama top. I took a deep breath, put my arm around her, then curled up beside her like a baby and went back to sleep.

When I woke up again, there was the smell of breakfast coming through the bedroom vents. Deborah turned over, smiled at me, and went back to sleep. I got up and went down stairs to see what magic had alerted my appetite.

Sammi was moving about the kitchen like she was on a mission.

"Sit down. I fixed you breakfast." Surrounded by sunlight coming through the windows over the counters, she looked like she was at home in the kitchen.

"Girl, I didn't even know you could cook," I said.

Sammi had been kind of quiet when she and Deborah first moved in with me. I tried to give her space. I knew how hard it could be for a fourteen-year-old to face her parents' divorce. I had counseled many students in dark times because of divorced parents over the years.

Sammi gave me a big hug. Nigerians are affectionate and easy to give hugs.

"Let me go put on some clothes," I said. I was barefoot in my pajama bottoms, but the smell of breakfast had lured me.

"Sit down," she said again. "I'm gonna give you something good." She was almost as pretty as Deborah. Her short natural hair framed a round face which looked like innocence before the Cross.

"You're fine, just as you are," she said. She handed me a plate with eggs, bacon, grits, biscuits, and jelly. She pressed a knife and fork in my hands.

I was ready for breakfast.

"Aren't you gonna have some, too?" I asked.

"No. I'm just gonna stand here and watch you," she said. Her big eyes seemed to take in everything. She looked different from the troubled young lady I'd been counseling at the middle school a few weeks ago when her mom and I first met, but I couldn't quite put my finger on the difference. Maybe it was the sunlight gently caressing her face.

The whistle went off on the coffee pot.

I stood up to get a cup for coffee.

"I got that," she said, and she moved to the counter before I did.

"I'll get it," I said. As I moved behind her, she backed into me, blocking me. She stretched her arm with the cup in her hand in front of her as far as she could reach. Laughing playfully as I reached for a coffee cup, she dropped the potholder she was holding to the floor. She turned facing me and stooped down to pick up the potholder.

The timer on the coffee pot sounded again.

"Good morning," said Deborah behind us.

I turned to face her.

"What's this?" Deborah asked.

"Breakfast," I said.

"No. I mean you two. What kind of game were you playing?"

"Would you like some breakfast, Mommy?" Sammi asked.

"Sure, baby. You made it?" she asked.

Yep. Just for you, and Big Man."

I cleared my throat. "I didn't even know she could cook," I said.

"Oh, she can cook," Deborah said. "Big Man, please put something on."

I went back upstairs to my bedroom. As I passed my dresser mirror, I saw that the sunlight through the windows let me see right through my pajama pants.

When I was getting out of my car at school on Monday, I had an eerie feeling I was going to fall or be hit by a falling object. I closed my car door and started towards the back stairs to my second floor counseling office. When I started up the stairs I could see a figure at the top of the landing.

"I know you're surprised to see me," my ex-wife, Angela, said.

I'd have been surprised but I'd given up being surprised by Angela.

"You waiting for me?" I asked.

"No. I was waiting for Godot or Jesus Christ, but since they don't seem to be coming anytime soon, I'd like to talk with you."

"About what, Angela?" It had been over three years now since we were divorced but she had been in my life constantly, it seemed.

"I don't know where to begin," she said. I looked her directly in the face and for the first time since I had known her, I absolutely believed her. Her beautiful face looked bewildered, but determined.

"Begin wherever you want, Angela, but I have five minutes before I'm supposed to be in my office inside."

"I'm going away, Big Man." She actually had the beginnings of tears in her eyes.

"Okay," I said. Angela wasn't going to pull me into anything.

"I have to ask you to do something."

"I hope it's legal."

"I want you to take care of our child."

"Our child?" Now, I knew she had lost it. Stone wacko. "Angela, we have been divorced for three years."

"I know. He's three," she said.

It'd been three years since Angela left me in Tucson, where she had crashed uninvited at my house. A lot had happened in that time. She had supposedly been engaged to her L. A. agent. She'd had an affair with my brother. And, all that time I had not seen her.

"Angela, you're not making any sense. But, it's been a long time since you made any sense," I said. I opened the back door and went into the hallway, leaving her standing there. I unlocked my office and went in, never looking back. Angela was saying something but I had completely tuned her out.

I sat down at the dinner table the next evening. "Why are you grumpy?" Deborah asked.

"Am I? Don't mean to be."

"You just have this dark, uninviting look." Deborah made me smile just to see her sitting across from me.

"Where's Sammi?" I asked.

"She'll be down as soon as she completely finishes her homework."

"She has to completely finish her homework before she can eat?" I asked.

"My father used to ask us at dinnertime 'What have you done today to deserve your dinner?' There were fourteen of us children. I think it was a good question. Besides, I don't want Sammi to have these crazy ideas American children have," she said.

"Like what?" I asked.

"Like they're equal to their parents. Like they're finding themselves. Sammi is not lost because I'm not lost. If she wants to know who she is, she can ask me."

"Young people today want to have a mind of their own," I said.

"Sammi can't have a mind of her own, because she has the mind I gave her."

"But now she lives in America, not Nigeria," I said.

"She lives in America, but Africa lives in her," Deborah said.

"Suit yourself," I said.

"You see, I said you were grumpy. Starting something that has no end, and ending something that has no beginning."

"What does that mean?"

"That I love you no matter what you think."

"And, you're going to do what you want to no matter what I say." I surprised myself.

"Hello, Big Man. The food looks good, Mommy." Sammi had a big smile, bright eyes, and a fresh, healthy glow as she entered the kitchen.

"Why so happy, Sammi?" I asked.

"Nothing. Just planning on having a nice day." She winked at me.

"Good for you. Think I'll join you," I said.

"Something bothering you, Big Man?" Deborah asked.

"Why do you think that?" I asked.

"You mumbled all night in your sleep." Deborah said.

"What did I say?"

"I don't speak sleep mumble," Deborah said.

"Okay."

"But you kept saying something about 'my son,' and somebody named Scooter, and how you were going back to see if he was dead."

"See if Scooter was dead? That's strange. But I don't remember dreaming."

"Dream time is clearing time, my grandmother used to say. Time to clear your mind of the ghosts that walk with you in the day. Who's Scooter?" Deborah waited.

"Scooter's my godson. He lives in Tucson. You'll meet him because he is coming here to stay a few days with us in a week."

"Coming here? How old is he?" Deborah asked.

"Sixteen," I said.

That evening Deborah seemed poised to jump on me. Everything I said got a snappy short okay-you-want-to-argue response, but I let it go by because my mind was preoccupied with Angela. Had she really lost her mind? But finally Deborah's responses got to me.

"What's going on?" I asked.

"What's going on? You have my daughter after you like a love-starved banshee."

What?" I asked. "I don't know what you're talking about."

"You are bringing a strange sixteen-year-old into the house with my thirteen-year-old daughter."

"Scooter is not a stranger," I said. "He's my godson."

"He may be your godson, but you admit that he's a man, albeit a young man, and I have a teenage daughter whose father left her solely in my care, who is hot to trot, and you bring in temptation on a plate. She can cook, all right. You walking around with everything exposed."

"What. Exposed?"

"Sammi was tantalized by looking through your pajamas the other morning while you pranced around naked."

"Deborah, what's gotten into us? We've never had an argument before."

"Well, I guess it is here. I'm going to have to leave. Sammi is my responsibility."

I looked up. Sammi was standing in the doorway to our bedroom. How long had she been there?

"Running out again, Mommy, just like you did on Dad?" Sammi looked like she was hurling a curse.

The doorbell rang. I looked out of the window. Angela's sports car was parked in the driveway.

"Damn. Double damn!" I said.

"Sammi, go to your room," Deborah said. Sammi did not move.

"You left Daddy because he was not good enough for you. You threaten Big Man like he's not good enough for you. You want to get rid of me because I love Big Man. You're nothing but trouble." Sammi's eyes were wide and fiery.

Deborah was on the other side of the room in one movement. She slapped Sammi across the face. Sammi did not move. The doorbell rang again.

All the way downstairs to the door my mind was in a wind tunnel searching for an anchor to hold onto. I opened the door. It wasn't Angela, but my ex-wife's crazy sister, Donna, who I had also dated. She had a child by the hand.

"Isn't that Angela's car?" I asked.

"Big Man, this is your son, Ray-Ray." She put the boy's hand in mine and moved away. The boy let out a loud scream and pulled away from me. Instinctively, I held on to his hand.

"Donna, what the hell's going on?"

"He's your son. Didn't you say you wanted a child? There he is. He needs a father. I bought the car from Angela." Donna turned and was gone. The boy was yelling, and Deborah and Sammi were arguing loudly upstairs.

Ray-Ray looked at me with quiet eyes as if to say, "What are you going to do now?" He had calmed down now and looked less intimidated by our being thrown together than I felt.

I stooped down to speak to him. He punched me in the face and ran behind the couch.

"Who are you? Some kind of monster?" I asked. I didn't run after him. The door was locked. He couldn't get out.

"What's going on?" Deborah asked. I was clutching my right eye and stooped over, when she got to the bottom of the step.

"I'm caught up in hell," I said. "The child is a demon."

"She's head-strong, like her father. She's growing up too fast. It's this American craziness she sees around her."

Ray-Ray came out from behind the couch, walking on his tippy toes, and looked at Deborah calmly.

"Who's this?" Deborah asked.

"I don't know," I said.

"Who was at the door?"

"It was Donna."

"Your old girlfriend, Donna? The sister of your old wife? Whatever." she said.

The boy climbed up on the couch and sat down. He looked like he was waiting to see what would happen next. I stood up. The three of us looked at each other. Ray-Ray stuck his thumb in his mouth, and grinned.

"Mom, what am I gonna do?" I asked. I had told my mother everything. I told her how Donna showed up at the house and abruptly deposited this three-year-old boy that Angela said was our son.

"Whats he look like?" Mom asked.

"Like a three-year-old, Mom. What kind of question is that?"

"Does he look like you?" she asked.

"How do I know? How do I know what I look like?"

"You look in a mirror from time to time, don't you? Does the boy look like you or not, Big Man?"

"Yes. Kinda."

"Does he walk on his toes?"

"Something like that."

"Big Man, God made it so a father can tell his child early on. Is he your child?"

"He could be." I hadn't expected to say that.

"Then, you know what to do. Bring him over here so I can put my arms around him and feed him some real food, man."

Ray-Ray settled in easy. He didn't cry. He could find anything to play with. His big eyes took in everything. But, he had to be watched so that nothing would happen to him. I had to figure out a plan. I needed answers. There was only one person who might be able to put me in forward gear. Lloyd.

Lloyd was the cousin of Donna, my ex-wife's half sister. It's complicated. But, we played enough basketball together in high school, knew and depended on each other when we both lived in New York, that I thought he could and would give me some answers about Ray-Ray. I'd called Angela's mother and she was as tight mouthed as a hungry gator on his lunch. She genuinely seemed in distress, like she really didn't know where Angela was. She acted like she had never seen Ray-Ray until Angela brought him to her house last week. Nothing was clear to her.

"Lloyd, tell me straight up what's going on," I said.

We were sitting in Clyde's bar. It was midday. All the early drunks had come and gone and the afternoon drunks had not pulled in yet. So, we had the dingy little shotgun bar all to ourselves. Clyde was watching a game on TV but he nodded every now and then.

"You tell me. Last thing I knew you were hot after my cousin Donna. Knew that was going to trip out. You never had luck with women. Look at me. Settled down with a honey. My queen. Life's good. Like Sunday morning."

"It's not always about you, Lloyd." I was a little irritated but I needed him, he didn't need me. "What's up with Angela? What's up with Donna? What's the story on the boy, Ray-Ray? The women say he's my son."

"You wanted a son, right?"

"But, I don't know what's going on."

"You mean you don't want to know what's going on. Maybe you can make nothing out of it. Maybe it makes you useful, and that scares the hell out of you."

"And, maybe you are getting off on giving me a hard time. I didn't ask for this." I gulped down my drink.

"Big Man, the world is not a tree stump for you to pee on. You get the women that you don't need, and then you need them when they have moved on. How you and the African princess?"

I felt my knuckles getting tight. I cocked my fist. I was getting pissed off with this overgrown narcissistic homeboy. I was thinking I might not get anything out of him because I might not be able to hold back off him.

"Lloyd, I'm happy you're married and settled. Deborah is good for me. She's intelligent, and well centered."

"You gon marry her?"

"Whoa. That's too far. I haven't even gotten that far."

"Well, why is she living with you then?"

"Man., I don't think I'm gonna answer that."

"No. You just want to pump me for information. You don't want to share anything. Never did. Big Man, you always thought you were better than everybody else. That's a fact."

It was getting hard for me to see, like blood was rushing from my brain into my eyeballs. I held to the edge of the bar.

"Wow, Lloyd. I didn't know that's how you felt about me."

"Me?" he said. "That's how everybody I know feels about you, Big Man."

"Then I'm getting a bum rap," I said. "'Cause I ain't like that at all."

"You'd get the same if you asked your own mother."

That's when I decked him. Knocked him completely from the bar stool. I stood over him. Looked down at him. And kicked him hard in the side while he was holding on to his jaw.

Clyde rushed over to us. He stood back sleepy-eyed as though he didn't want to wake up. I put a $20 bill down on the counter.

"I'll pay for the drink," I said. I turned and started out of the bar while Lloyd was drawing up next to the bar stool he had been sitting on.

Later that night my mother called.

"Where are you?" she asked.

"I'm drowning in Lake Mayer."

"Don't try to be smart, Big Man. I been on the phone all afternoon. Angela has disappeared. Run off somewhere. She's ill. Has stage four cancer. Her crazy sister, Donna, took everything of hers or she gave it to her. The child is yours. Angela didn't want to tell you but she had to. I dredged it out of her mother. That woman was never too smart. That's why she took so much abuse from Angela's father. Now, bring that boy over here so I can take a look at my grandson. Where is he?"

"Mom. Thanks. He's at my next-door neighbors, playing with her kids."

"Get him over here so I can put some grandma loving on him, you hear? You can bring that Deborah and her little fresh pot daughter, too, for dinner. I think I can look at them today. Long as we don't make it a habit."

"Mom, you are as good as gold."

"God has blessed me with another son. And, with the same name as your brother Raymond. Don't think I'm not grateful."

"Thank you, Mom."

"You better thank God. Oh, and Angela's mother is coming by in a few minutes. She got the birth certificate and everything on the boy. Thought I'd get everything while I could."

I drove like I was going to the emergency room to get home. The adrenaline was pumping through my system and I felt a sense of joy swelling up in me.

As I pulled up to my driveway, I saw Deborah standing in the doorway talking to two police officers. First thing that came to my mind was 'We've been robbed.' But my feeling of joy still engulfed me. Two police cars were parked on the curb in front of my house.

"Mr. Johnson?" the police officer asked.

"Yes. What's going on?"

"We need you to come down to the police station with us, sir. Got some questions to ask you." Deborah didn't move from the front door.

"Ask me. What questions? Ask me whatever questions you have to ask me. Ask me now."

"No, sir. We prefer to do it down at the police station. I'd like for you to get in the car now. Don't want to have to handcuff you or make a scene."

The police car was hot. The officer didn't turn the air on and I was having trouble breathing. Knew it was stress but knowing it and being able to do something about it is different. The bars that separated the front seat from the back seat seemed like a cage. The doors were locked from the front of the car. I tried to think about it calmly but the feeling of being closed in, out of control was taking my breath away.

"Rape? Somebody is out of their mind," I said.

"Her mother has pressed charges. The girl's been examined. She's been penetrated. You want to tell us what happened?"

"I'll tell you what happened. I let a crazy woman in my house, and her crazy daughter. That's what happened."

My mother didn't have that I told-you-so look on her face when she watched me collect my wallet and keys at the police station window. She was somber but nonjudgmental.

"I'm sorry I had to get you to come down here," I said.

"That's what mothers are for. To pick up the pieces when the games are over," she said. "I don't think you will be coming back here."

We quietly went through the police station doors into the evening air.

"I brought Ray-Ray to the house. We had a nice talk. Well, I had a nice talk. That boy is the spitting image of you. Don't know why Angela kept him from you. From everybody. 'Cept she was always jealous that you had too much. Now, I feel sorry for her."

"Sorry for her? All I ever wanted was a family. Wife to make a life with. Children. We could have had that, me and Angela."

"You can't have what you can't have until it's time. Maybe it's time now," Mom said.

"Why did she do this, Mom? Why did Deborah press charges against me? For rape? That's crazy."

"Your life is getting cleaned up. She's out of your house. Your sister and I saw to that. She and her little tramp daughter. I told my lawyer, Tim Burns, to tell her that I would have you press charges against her for false accusations and she'd be sued in court. And, she has to pay all the court costs if she was wrong."

"She's a lawyer."

"Maybe she didn't learn that she's not above the law. By the time she finished with that daughter of hers, everything came out. The girl lied that you had raped her. She is pregnant by some guy in school. She had just had sex with him on the way home from school. Her momma examined her. In the girl's mind, if she told her mother you raped her, they would leave your house and you'd be blamed for it. Crazy but there it is. They are both out of there now."

"I thought Deborah was the one."

"Now you have a son. That's enough for one season."

-9-

AN OLD LOVE

I rode in the narrow elevator cage alone up to the 11th floor. My ascent was a slow, rickety song of metal against metal accompanied by the lingering smells of slices of uncelebrated humanity that had gone up before me. I rang the bell at 11C. I stood back from the peep hole in the dark green door. All of the opening conversations I'd rehearsed in my head on the flight from Savannah to New York and on the way over to this Brooklyn apartment building evaporated into nothingness.

Angela opened the door. She looked neither surprised nor bothered by my unexpected arrival.

"Come on in," Angela said.

I followed her into an apartment I'd never been in. The furniture from the time when we were married stared back at me like children separated from a cousin.

"How are you doing?" I asked.

Except for slightly dark circles around her sparkling eyes, Angela looked well. She hadn't lost any weight. In jeans and a t-shirt she was as curvaceous as ever. The cancer had not taken a toll on her physical beauty. But it was her emotional state in which I was most interested. How was she coping with a diagnosis of stage four cancer? How was she emotionally in the midst of an uncertain certainty?

"I figured you'd come. How's my Ray-Ray?" she said. I could hear a throaty despondency when she said our son's name.

"Just like his momma. Self-determined and can't stay still."

I felt sad, sensing what it must be like for Angela to miss our three-year-old son.

"I think about him every minute," she said. "Sit down before I take you in my arms and hold you real tight."

"You can do that, Angela. I can handle it."

"Question is, can I?" she said.

I spent the afternoon with Angela talking about our childhood in Savannah, our crazy friends who have gotten crazier as the years passed, and the ups and downs of our ten-year marriage. She got more and more relaxed, more like her old self, but there were moments when a quietness would descend upon her.

"How is your mom?" she asked.

"She's got a new love in her life," I said.

"Get outta here," she exclaimed.

"Ray-Ray," I said. "Mom's replaced all three of her sons with Ray-Ray, and Ray-Ray thinks Mom is the center of the world."

Angela's face became gray. I could feel how hard it was for her to think of our son, and not have him with her.

"Does he ask…?" she started.

"He misses you," I said. "We show him your picture every day and call your name. He kisses the picture."

"I think I did the right thing." She looked away for a moment. "What do you think?" she asked. "About sending him to you."

"He's my son." I said.

Angela looked at me as though reading a page. "Are you sure?" she asked.

I hesitated. "Yes, I'm sure."

"Because you saw the birth certificate?" she asked.

"Because his body temperature is the same as mine," I said.

"You sure he's not your brother Raymond's?" she asked.

"Raymond's skin was cold. But it was good of you to name him Raymond," I said.

"But, maybe I shoulda told you about him when he was born," she said.

"It's done now, Angela. We can let it go."

"You were always good at letting things go, Big Man. Wasn't easy keeping it from everybody. New Yorkers don't ask questions. I never took him to Savannah. That wouldn't have worked."

"I try not to bring trouble, that's all. Angela, I'll be here as long as you need me," I said.

In the week that I spent in Brooklyn, I visited Angela every afternoon, and stayed with her until evening set in. I took her to the hospital twice for her chemo, and I tried to keep her mind positive.

The Saturday before I was to return home to Savannah, Angela surprised me.

"Can you take me to church tomorrow?"

"You wanna go to church?" I asked. Angela and I hadn't been to church together since we were first married and living at home in Savannah. We never went to church the nine and a half years we lived in New York.

"Let's go to Daddy Grace's in Harlem," she said.

"Way up in Harlem? Sure you have the strength for the trip?"

"I want to eat some fried chicken. Some greens, potato salad and chocolate layer cake."

"You want to pig out," I said. "Ain't nothing wrong with you girl."

"Nothing a little loving won't cure. Stay tonight," she said.

"And?" I asked.

"And what?" she asked.

"Angela, you got something in mind?" I said. I remembered her early morning visits to share my bed after we were divorced, and her long stay at my place in Tucson. Was that all she needed from me?

"And, whatever," she said.

I took her in my arms and held her. The time between that moment and the first time I had held her in the playground behind the school when we were fourteen slipped away. That moment was newness, light and warmth. Then, a feeling crept into the back of my mind like a hand reaching across my brain and squeezing it tight. The feeling lingered a moment, then disappeared.

When I got back to the apartment where I was staying with my cousin, I felt like I was walking a half inch off the floor. I hummed as I packed my clothes. I'd not be coming back because my flight to Savannah was early Monday morning. I'd be spending the night with my first sweetheart, the woman by whom all my other women had been measured.

I picked up two huge gyros on my way back to Angela's. If Angela was hungry, I was gonna be sure she got stuffed. On the subway I began to hear voices in the muffled metallic whirring of the train. The voices merged into one sound of speaking that reverbed in my head. I always thought that spirits run in everything but the train hadn't made itself speak until then. Maybe too much intensity with my attention to Angela had brought me to a place of vulnerability to things unseen. I tried to shut the voice out. A short, heavy-set, shiny-faced black woman with a mustache, deep red lips, and thick, tangled mixed gray dreadlocks, standing holding onto a post frowned at me like she was God. A tall, rail-thin old white man near the woman laughed aloud shrilly in harmony with the voice that spoke in the whir of the train. Something was about to happen and I didn't have a clue. The universe sometimes prepares us for tricks.

With my small duffle bag and my bag of gyros, I crossed the street to Angela's apartment just as an ambulance siren blasted, pulling away from the front of her building. I went into the building's noisy, crowded lobby. An elderly lady I had spoken to earlier in the week took me by the arm.

"That was the lady in 11C, where you were visiting," she said.

"You mean… Angela, in the ambulance?" I asked.

"And, are you her husband?" the nurse on the desk asked. She didn't wait for an answer. "Through those double doors, first door on the right," she said.

Angela was sitting up in bed. A calm expression was on her face. Inside I wanted to die. I did not want to lose her.

"You all right?" I asked. I took her hands. They were warm, familiar. I kissed her on the cheek.

"I was just thinking to tell you something that may surprise you when you walked in," she said.

"Okay. You're in the intensity ward. Rushed here in an ambulance and you sitting up here thinking to surprise me?"

"A girl should always have surprises."

"What did the doctors say, Angela?" I asked.

"Oh, they are running some tests. I feel fine. Don't like ambulances. Everybody seems to have something to do except the person being hustled around at breakneck speed."

"What happened?"

"I went down to the lobby to get the paper. Apparently I fell out on the floor."

"Did you hurt yourself?"

"Only thing hurt, far as I could tell, was my pride 'cause I didn't have on any make-up and was in my sweats. Woman gotta look good for whatever. Especially, if there's gonna be people all around suffocating you with questions. I was planning on a nice, sexy evening with you, and I couldn't even get myself together."

"You're always together, whatever that is, enough for me." I squeezed her hand.

"Big Man, do you know I have never been with another man? In my whole life. You're the only man I have known. Oh, I loved Raymond but that was puppy love. We became best friends, especially after he became addicted to drugs. He didn't have anybody. Nobody he could trust."

I don't know why I wanted to shut what she was saying out. But I knew my job was to make Angela feel good.

"I'm gonna cancel my flight back to Savannah, Angela. I'm gonna stay right here with you. I called your mother and she said you'd already called her."

"You don't have to stay. I'll be all right. I'd rather you be with our son."

"There's always time to be with Ray-Ray. Now, I want to be where you need me," I said.

"I need you with our son. I'll be all right. Probably be out of here by Monday. You know insurance companies don't want you to have time to get comfortable in the hospitals. Plus, my sister always says people get sicker in hospitals. Being a nurse, Donna ought to know."

I didn't want to think about Donna. Had tried to block the crazy times I had dating her on my mind.

"She didn't love you, you know. She just always wanted my toys. She was always like that."

"What did the doctors say? Why'd you faint?" I didn't know if I wanted the answer.

"Said they'd know when they get the tests back. Maybe they will, maybe they won't. I'm not really afraid of dying, Big Man. It's kinda like the time my mother baked brownies, cut them up in squares, stacked them one on top of the other in a cake dish. She put them on top of the refrigerator. She said we'd have them in the evening as dessert. My brothers and I hit those brownie squares until they got down to two. I saw those last two in the cake dish and said to myself, 'I might as well eat the last two, I'm gonna get murdered anyway when Mom finds out they are all gone.' Life is like that. Might as well go with it."

"I don't believe that. Y'all ate all your momma's brownies."

"And they were good."

"Shame. Shame. Shame."

"Yeah. We were greedy and reckless, and we knew there would be a price to pay but we kept on. I gotta keep on, Big Man. I ain't scared."

"I'm scared. Who's gonna sleep in my bed?"

"Oh, you'll find somebody. And, I hope she'll make you very happy. You deserve to be happy, Big Man. You are a good man. The best I've ever known, my whole life." The tears began to flow from her eyes. I leaned down and kissed her tears.

"I was jealous, Big Man. Every woman wanted you. Those gray eyes. That sexy swag. I couldn't keep up with the eyeballs always zooming in on you."

"I didn't see all that."

"I know. That's what made it so cute. But it was trouble."

"Are you trying to flatter me after all this time?"

A tall, thin Mediterranean-looking doctor with eyebrows that matched Salvador Dali's thick, curled-up whiskers entered the room. His eyes were also Dalian, wide, kinda of crazy and spooky.

"How's my patient?" he asked. "How are you, sir?" He extended his hand.

"How is your patient?" I shook his hand.

"We won't have all the tests in until Monday. So we will keep you comfortable until then. I've looked over your records that we pulled in from your doctor. Will let you know everything bright and early Monday morning." He smiled an I'm-on-my-way smile and left.

On the flight to Savannah I kept seeing the face of the short, fat black woman on the train. And hearing the shrill laughter of the thin old white man echo in the whir of the plane. I could not hear the words but something was being said.

"There ain't nothing God and me can't handle," Mom said.

She was fussing over Ray-Ray's hair like she was a big time cosmetologist. Ray-Ray was being indulgent like he was used to the routine. He was snuggly, his back pushed up against her, playing with a miniature robot. I remembered how wicked she could be with a hair brush. She brushed all the shine out of my hair as a kid. It looked like the same brush, too, a weapon of terror.

"Don't brush his hair so hard, Mom."

"He at least stands still. Not like you. He's got pretty hair, too. Good hair."

"All hair is good, Mom, if it keeps your head warm," I said.

"I been praying for Angela. Praying mighty hard. Poor girl. How is she handling it? Cancer ain't nobody's pushover. 'Bout time they found a cure for it. Been killing people since ancient Egypt."

"How do you know that, Mom?"

She stopped brushing the nonchalant Ray-Ray's hair and put the brush on a side table.

"There, Ray-Ray. You look better than your daddy." She looked at me with that devilish grin of hers. "You think I don't read. We have lost a lot of family to cancer. I read. Stay up with me. But don't try to get ahead of me cause it might be bumpy." Mom was fun when she was feisty. She was fun anyway.

"How's he been behaving?"

Ray-Ray looked like he was starting to get used to having conversations about him around him. He perked up to hear but looked like he was trying not to seem too interested.

"He's been fine. We get along just fine, don't we, Ray-Ray? I might even start shooting some hoops with you, Ray-Ray, so you can be a basketball player like your daddy was. Would you like that, Ray-Ray?" Ray-Ray nodded his head and continued to contort his toy robot.

"He's a good kid. And good-looking like his momma. And smart like his momma. Only thing he got like his daddy is his appetite. Let me go fix my men some good food for lunch."

"Mom, you sure know how to hurt a guy."

"Big Man, this boy is just like you in every way. It's like somebody took you and shrunk you. He even got your sexy gray eyes."

"Mom, you think I got sexy eyes? You never said that before."

"Big Man, your daddy had sexy gray eyes. If he hadn't, there wouldn't have been you, and your brothers and Sheila. And there wouldn't been my Ray-Ray. Come on, Ray-Ray, let Grandma fix her boys some food."

There were never shadows around my mom. Her house was always blessed and she never brought trouble. She weathered storms with the same calm as she baked a chicken or sliced a ham.

I kept calling Angela at the hospital all day Monday, but got no answer. I tried the front desk and was told that she was not in the ICU anymore. She had been moved, but they didn't seem to be able to locate her. I spent as much time with Ray-Ray as I could. Despite what Mom had said about him being like me, when I looked at Ray-Ray, I saw Angela. Angela was a spirit caught up in his spirit, fresh and new, written all over him.

Ray-Ray did have my appetite, though. In the evening at my house, I made a plate of homemade French Fries – not the paper-tasting McDonald's or frozen sawdust variety, but real potatoes cut in the kitchen, seasoned and deep fried – and set them down with rich, red tomato ketchup. A huge plate for the two of us. Ray-Ray almost matched me hand for hand digging into those fries. He also laughed and smiled easily. I was still finding myself a little afraid of getting too close to him because I still could not believe he was in the world. A son. A gift from God.

We went over to my sister Sheila's house for a visit later. Sheila had already spoiled Ray-Ray. As soon as we went in the house he went to a box of toys and began to pull things out.

"Hey, wait, Ray-Ray," I said. "You can't just take things like that. You have to ask permission."

That's all right," Sheila said. "Aunt Sheila made that toy box just for Ray-Ray."

Ray-Ray took the toys he had in hands and jumped up in Sheila's lap like a co-conspirator in some intrigue.

"Oh, it's like that," I said. "I'm gone for a few days, and you take over my son. Spoil him."

"I spoiled you, too, Big Man, so don't even try it," Sheila said.

She was right. Being the only girl out of the four of us, and the second oldest, next to me, she spoiled everybody.

"So, how is Angela dealing with things?" Sheila asked. Ray-Ray had scuttled off to a corner stacking wooden blocks.

"I haven't been able to catch up with her at the hospital. Apparently, they have moved her out of ICU, but I can't get a line on where she is. Can you imagine hospitals losing people?"

"Hospitals are warehouses. They lose inventory all the time, though they charge you a butt and a bosom for every trinket they give you. If she's out of

ICU, then she's either in a less serious section, which is good, or she's been sent home. That may or may not be good. What did the doctors tell you before you left?"

"That they were running some tests. Would know more when they got the results back, which should have been this morning."

"I know this is hard on you. Angela, the divorce, the secret about Ray-Ray."

"Yeah. It's kinda hard, Sheila."

"Mom said when Dad died, 'God took away from me what he gave me. At least he gave me love.'"

I said, "I see that love right before me in Ray-Ray."

"What are you going to do?" Sheila asked.

"I'm going in your kitchen and find a feast in your refrigerator," I said.

"You'd better hold off 'cause if you don't eat a ranch when you go back by Mom's, she'll scalp you. It's good of you to let Mom keep Ray-Ray for while. That's good for you, but Big Man, that's your son, get somebody to live in with you – now that your Nigerian girlfriend and her demon daughter are gone – and raise your child in your house. I think that's what Angela would want."

My cell phone went off with the theme song from "Shaft."

"Angela. I've been trying to find you," I said. It was like Sheila had spoken Angela into calling. She was talking fast. I was listening, and playing back in my head what she was saying in a rapid speed.

I finally got my playbacks analyzed and she gave me a moment of silence.

"That can't be," I said. "But it is. That's fantastic. Unbelievable. Everything is possible, isn't it? Everything I'm so happy. Oh, baby, I don't know what to say. I'm coming to New York."

I flipped my cell shut. I was flabbergasted.

"That was Angela? What did she say?" Sheila asked.

"You wouldn't believe it. I don't believe it," I said.

"What? Do I have to choke you to get it out of you?"

I still could not bring myself to say what Angela had told me. I saw the fat black woman with the mustache from the subway sitting in the chair across from me, and I heard the tall, thin white man laughing behind her. I noticed now that he looked like Moses. But all the images I'd ever seen of Moses, he was fat. Why would he be fat in the wilderness when the people were starving?

"She said the tests showed she didn't have cancer," I said.

"What? I thought she was told she had stage four cancer. You don't misdiagnose that," Sheila said.

"All I know is, now she is being told she doesn't have it, and that's good enough for me," I said.

The black mustached woman in the chair winked at me. The thin Moses had stopped laughing and had a smile on his face. Then a light cut through them and they were gone.

"What are you gonna do?" Sheila asked.

"Daddy, can you make this for me?" Ray-Ray asked. He held up four Legos.

"What do you want to make?" I asked. He had called me Daddy.

My life had been up and down, but Mom, Sheila, my brothers, and Angela had been on the up side of things. Was I being given another chance to bring the down up with Angela?

"Invite Angela to come and stay with you 'til you figure things out," Mom said. She took the news of Angela's misdiagnosis as a sign from God almost like she was in on it. Mom with her fashion plate wardrobe twenty-four seven didn't look anything like the fat black woman that haunted my day dreamscape. Mom was too fly and svelte to look like that, and too lively to sit around inhabiting people's thoughts.

"I don't know, Mom. It's complicated and getting more complicated by the day. When I don't know what to do, I prefer to do nothing, like Daddy always said."

"I never paid any attention to your father doing nothing. I either found a way to get him to do what needed to be done, or I did it myself. Bring that girl home, I tell you."

"Can't do that, Mom. It doesn't feel right."

Mom cleared her throat. "If you don't get this right, you'll regret it." She started humming and polishing furniture. Mom always cleaned her house to usher in a new attitude. We kids knew this well, being the little army she deployed to make the changes that swept and polished the old haunts out of her realm.

That night changed my life. At least, it stopped it cold and gave me a slap that will never leave me as long as I live.

"Is this Gary Johnson?" asked the voice on my cell.

"Yes, and who is this?" There was only a number on my phone log, no contact name.

"Mr. Johnson, your information is the only information we have on file and you are listed as next of kin."

"Who is this? What is this about?"

"This is Graham Salem. I'm the information officer at the hospital where your wife was a patient."

I'm beginning now to need more air.

"This morning, Mr. Johnson, your wife was being discharged from the hospital. A nurse went down to the hospital discharge entrance with her as one usually does. Your wife was in a wheelchair for the discharge. Just as she was getting out of the wheelchair to say goodbye to the nurse, an out-of-control truck careened into the two of them. Your wife was killed, sir."

The funeral was very short. I kept seeing faces I recognized but was only seeing them on the periphery of my consciousness. My family, Angela's family. Her mother, her half sister, Donna, Lloyd, BeeBee, and Cynthia, and lots of people I hadn't seen since Angela and I were sweethearts in junior high school. The sun refused to shine. The birds were chirping at the grave site and the threat of a thunderstorm seemed kept at bay.

I held Ray-Ray's hand but not too tight. We both would need gentleness and strength for the times ahead.

-10-

A STRANGE RIVER

Ray-Ray made a sniffling sound. The seabirds flying over the Savannah River were having a circus above us. I threw a stone in the water. I watched the stone skip along the surface, then, dunked into the blue, disappear abruptly. Ray-Ray had a cold, an ear infection or a stuffy nose almost every week. I didn't remember having anything but an annual sniffle when I was a kid.

Ray-Ray chose a stone from the ground like a priest looking for virtue in the dirt. With all his strength, he chunked it out as far as he could throw. The stone plunked into the waiting water. Ray-Ray looked more and more like my father. My father was a mystery. He was ever present but I did not know him. I don't think my sister and brothers ever knew him, either. I am not sure what Mom knew; she knew him before he was man enough to be a father. Since Ray-Ray's mother had died, he seemed more solemn. Was this normal for a three-year-old? I have a lot to learn. Ray-Ray was still welcoming of all of us around him, but it seemed a part of him had locked itself up somewhere.

"Here Ray-Ray, take this." I put the small nasal inhaler up to his nose and sprayed a whiff of the spray into his nostrils.

"Wanna go home." He looked up at me as though I could whisk him away in a puff and be at home.

"You don't like the river?" I asked.

"Ye-us." He sounded like he didn't want to embarrass the river as he stood on its banks.

"You don't like the white seagulls, the diving cranes, the sky birds?" I asked. A crane flew close to the bank, then darted back over the river, its neck outstretched.

"Where's train?" he asked.

"I said 'crane.' See that dark bird over there?" I point in the sky to our right.

"No," he said.

"You don't see it?" I stooped beside him and pointed to the sky. The white cranes with red necks like markings on bowling pins were making a spectacle over the river.

"Wanna go home," he said.

He was like Angela. When his mind was made up, there was no distracting him. He sniffled some more. It was the fresh air along the river that made me bring him out. I wanted to share the fresh air and the smell of the rich, black dirt. I wanted him to see the tall, stately brown cattails. The Savannah marshes along the riverside seemed to offer renewal. They were fed by incoming tides and drainage from the river, and were rich with birds, other animals and plants. The cordgrass grew in tall, dense masses, sending roots into the salty depths of the marshland.

Ever since Angela was killed in a freak accident leaving the hospital in New York, I had tossed in my bed thinking of her each night. I learned more about her the few days before she died than I had known having grown up together, and then being married to her for almost ten years.

Death gives us gaps in life that we may never fill. I spent my whole life in the house with my father and never really knew him, either. But, unlike Angela, I did not have any questions until after he was dead. Maybe, coming out to the river was more for me than it was for Ray-Ray. Maybe I needed the open air, and a time and place for answers to come on their own.

"Okay. Let's go home." I took Ray-Ray by the hand and led him back up the slope of the riverbank. We turned from the Savannah River, that ran as wildly and majestically as it pleased, narrowing in some places but deep enough for the tall ships carrying the Olympic torch to pass once. It was here long before people brought their confusions, dreams and misgivings, building their lives and livelihoods upon its banks.

There was always talk of widening the river's channel. The channel had been good enough for the Native Americans. They had built settlements on its bluffs and the channel had provided them with food for generations. It was wide enough for the slave ships to come up the river bringing death, horror, and a black human cargo, ushering in a still dangerously poised promise of racial conflict. But it was not deep enough to see the future progress the planners of the city foresaw as Savannah sat elegantly quaint, wrapped in Spanish moss, and guarded by huge live oak trees. There were questions to be asked of the river.

Ray-Ray's face lit up when I drove into my mother's driveway.

"Did you have a good time with your daddy, Ray-Ray?" Mom asked.

"Yes, ma'am." Ray-Ray picked up a sandwich from the tray of sandwiches Mom brought out to the back patio. He walked out into the back yard nibbling on the big sandwich in his hand.

"Why don't you let him spend a few days with me, Big Man?" Mom asked.

"So you can spoil him some more?" I asked.

"Spoiled you, didn't I? That's what I do. But I was thinking more like giving you a break. Angela has only been dead two weeks, and you haven't stopped moving. You're just like your father."

"What was my father like? I didn't know the man. He was just here. He said things but I don't know what he was like."

"What do you mean, Big Man? I don't understand where that came from," Mom said.

"He was here, but you did everything. Now, I don't know who he was. I think I want Ray-Ray to know who I am," I said.

"Are you accusing me of something? If you are, I don't know what it is."

"Oh, forget it, Mom. I probably don't know what I'm saying."

"Or, maybe you are saying it clearly, Big Man. On second thought, what it sounds like to me is that you are saying I got in the way of you knowing your father. Is that it? If that's it, you are right."

"I am?"

"You got to know enough of him to make you want to be something in this life. To make you act like a man. To make you not be a selfish, self-centered, conniving, lying…"

"Wow. Where is all that coming from?"

"I was trying to protect you. Protect you, and Sheila, and Raymond and Teddy, all of you children. You got to know enough of your father not to need to know anymore. I knew it all, do you hear? I knew it all."

"What, Mom? What is it that you knew that we didn't know?"

"Still, I couldn't stop it. It must have been in the blood. His blood was in your brothers. His mind's in yours. Thank God for Sheila, she's like me."

"Mom, I just realized that I didn't know anything about him. Oh, yeah, we sat down at the table together to have dinner, but you did the talking. He only said what you asked him to say. That's what I seem to remember. I just started to know that I didn't really know him."

"You knew all you needed. I knew him."

Ray-Ray came back up on the patio. He tugged at my arm as my mother took a napkin and reached down to wipe the mustard from around his mouth.

"Wanna go home," he said.

When Angela walked towards me on our wedding day, my heart shifted into idle, my palms became wet, my breathing halted, and I felt like everyone around me could see me standing there as though I were naked. The wind settled into a calm breeze and the sky turned a clear light blue mist. Angela was a woman in soft white, surrounded by the daylight's glimmering. That moment was the tying time between the day I first laid eyes on Angela in second grade and the day I asked her to go to the teen dance in ninth grade;

it was the culmination of a thousand hugs and smiles we had shared. It was our wedding day, and it was made in Heaven.

I could feel my face beaming with pride like it was light brighter than the daylight. I wanted someone to share that moment with. I glanced over at my father, sitting next to my mother, in a three-piece gray suit and deep blue tie. My father, dark brown, looked up at me from the folding chair where he sat on the lawn. I could imagine the elixir of Old Spice shaving lotion that made me think of manhood when I was around him as a boy. There was a look on his face that was unfathomable. What was supposed to be the look on the face of the father of the groom on his son's wedding day? I did not see a smile on my father's face. I turned back to Angela. She was so pretty. I could feel my chest swell up. I remember thinking, "This is it." But, 'it' had no name that I could call. I was happy. I had to stand like a man victorious in love, wanting the prettiest girl he'd ever known coming towards him to say that nobody and nothing would ever take her away from him. Now, she was dead. There was an empty place in my heart. From the happiest day of my life, the time had changed in so many unforeseeable ways.

That was a lifetime ago. Time had stolen Angela from me. She was locked now in a time past. My father, too, was locked in time past. How little I knew of him. It is like I am watching this river of life passing and not knowing the mysteries it holds. It will not pass again.

"You feelin' betta, Ray-Ray?" I heard myself speaking in this little kid fake voice that adults use when they want to make children comfortable. Ray-Ray looked at me like he was trying to figure something out.

"You okay, Ray-Ray?" I stopped that kid's voice because it was weird and probably made Ray-Ray think I was ill.

"Wanna see the birds?" Ray-Ray said.

"What birds?" I asked.

"Sky birds," he said.

"The birds by the river, diving in and out of the water, like the other day?" I asked.

"Un huh," he said.

"Don't say 'Un huh,' Ray-Ray, talk like a big person. You're a big person, right?"

"No," Ray-Ray said.

"Tomorrow, Ray-Ray, we'll go down to the river. We'll see the sky birds, okay?"

"Oh-kay," he said. We went home, my son and me, to a house that seemed waiting for something. I put Ray-Ray's pajamas on him, and helped him brush his teeth. I tucked him in bed, just as my mother tucked me, Sheila, Raymond and Teddy in bed at night when we were kids. I don't remember my father ever saying "Goodnight" to us.

Impulsively, on the way home from work the next day, I drove out to my father's grave in the bright Savannah sun. Laurel Grove Cemetery was home to many parts of the history of Savannah. The lives of men and women are deposited in their graves and their headstones summarize their brief walk in the sunlight.

"You always said I didn't know how to keep Angela," I said. I looked down to where the remains of my father were buried.

The gray headstone stood silent to my words.

"I never knew what you meant, Dad." I did not expect an answer. I'd come because I was not afraid to ask questions. The breeze stirred in the trees above the gravesite. Generations of my father's family were nestled there together in the grassy mound, keeping silent company for all eternity. How many of the fathers had shared themselves with their sons? How many of them had wrapped themselves in themselves and gone silently off into the night of Death? I was beginning to realize that my visits to my father's grave, though not frequent, were about asking questions that seemed closed. Because he was no longer above ground did not mean that the ground had swallowed my questions. Who was this man, my father, and why did I know nothing about him? I lived in his house, ate his food, but I did not know him.

I met my high school classmate, BeeBee, at Walmart. I was surprised to see him back in Savannah. The last time I'd seen him was at a wedding of our classmate and fellow basketball team member, Lloyd, and before then, in Tucson, Arizona where he and his kooky wife Cynthia and demon son, Jonathan, lived. He was coming down the long store aisle towards me. Preoccupied with looking on the shelves, he didn't see me. I ducked through a break in the aisle over into the other aisle. When I turned around, BeeBee appeared right in front of me.

"Hey, Big Man, you are a sight for sore eyes." He reached his hand out to high-five me, then quickly turned that greeting into a rigorous embrace.

Before I could breathe out, he pushed me back from his embrace and was staring me in the face as if he were a holy man about to make an absolution.

"I hope you aren't blaming yourself for Angela's death," he said.

BeeBee's words stung. Until then I had never thought that I might be blaming myself for Angela's death. Sure, things would have been different if I had never left her alone in the hospital in New York. Things might have been different if I had never left New York and had gone to pick her up when she was discharged from the hospital. But, Angela was the one who had wanted me to come back to Savannah to be with our son, and I was also feeling guilty about leaving Ray-Ray in Savannah when we had only just gotten to know each other.

"I know you don't think much of me and Cynthia anymore, but we always loved you and Angela. We thought y'all were the perfect couple. We always envied you guys. So good-looking, so smart." BeeBee looked like he was about to have tears in his eyes. All I could think was that this butt-hole and his wife had once had me arrested in New York for cutting off their coat sleeves in retaliation for them cutting off the pants of my perfectly good blue suit so it would fit their idiot son for the funeral of a cousin they didn't really care about. It all came rushing back to me with alarming speed.

"Don't sweat it, BeeBee. How are you and your family?" I changed my tone of speaking to put a moat between us as I spied my exit point. "Good seeing you, home. Tell Cynthia I said 'Hi.'"

That quickly I was out of a coming storm within my head. Did he think he could own my feelings just by speaking them into existence with his crazy workaholic, wife-abused mind?

When I left Walmart I headed straight to my sister's.

"Sheila, do you think I think I am in any way responsible for Angela's death? I asked.

Sheila sat quiet for a moment in the big chair in her living room her hefty husband usually sat in when he was home. I sat across from her waiting for her answer to confirm my idea that what I had asked wasn't true.

"Yes. You were not at fault, but you think you were."

"Why do you say that?" Again, I was stunned. It was like BeeBee had taken over her body and uttered nonsense through Sheila's lips. "You don't really believe that, do you, Sheila?"

"Why do you always ask people things, and then when you get the answer, you want it changed? Do you want me to say, 'No, Big Man, I don't think you blame yourself for your wife's death.'? Then what, Big Man?"

"Then… then I'd know you understood, Sheila."

"Big Man, I know you loved Angela. We all know you loved Angela. We knew ever since the two of you were teenagers. But, I know you can't let go of that feeling 'What if… what would have happened to Angela.' It was a truck, out of control, plowing into her on a street in New York when you were in Savannah with your son. You can't hold yourself responsible, no more than the tide cannot not come in or the Savannah River can change its course."

I wanted to slap Sheila. I had never hit my sister. I had always been there for her growing up. I never let anyone take advantage of Sheila. I'd fight anyone in school or anywhere else who did anything wrong to my sister. Now, I wanted to slap her. I got up from her oversized chair and walked toward her front door.

"See, you are just like your father. You never have anything to say when you need to have something to say. You just walk away."

"Our father, Sheila. I really want to slap you. And, you are doing the same thing Mom always did, knowing everything and being in charge. Maybe, just maybe, our father didn't have anything to say because Mom always had the answers, always had everything under control."

"No, Big Man. Our father didn't have anything to say most of the time because he was a drunk. A functioning drunk, but a stand-up drunk everyday of our lives. It was all he could do to smile that weird smile of his and look off in the distance. Mom kept him looking good so we would look like a well adjusted family, but we were not. Slap me? You would even think to slap me. You would even let that out of your mouth."

What had I done? What had I said? Sheila had always been there for me too.

"I'm sorry, Sheila," I said.

"Yes. You are." She stood straight up and walked out of the living room of her own house and disappeared.

The women in the family were always the most dramatic – not diva overwrought drama, but soap opera worked to the tears. My mother could give three roles in one half hour with no sign of transition from one side of her character palate to another. I guess my brothers and I were like my father in that we never modulated out of a studied range. Did we get that from my father or was it something built in with being a black man raised in Savannah? Sheila and Mom had had their say. Stripped of the drama, they were honest women, and they had no reason to lie to me or mislead me. What they said was what they thought. I could take it or leave it. One thing I liked about the Johnson women was their economy with drama. You got it, you got it straight, and there weren't any repeats.

I took Ray-Ray down to the Savannah River the next afternoon after I came home from school. He wanted to see the "sky birds." I wanted to let him have what he wanted. I wanted to be there with him as he saw the world create itself before him in a thousand ways every hour of the day. His mother could not share the joy of seeing him see what life was made of, but I would try to be her eyes in this world. I would keep watch and I would watch over the gift that Angela had left me, our son.

Ray-Ray was sparkle and light in his matching blue shirt and shorts. Mom and Sheila did shop well for him and I was always amazed that he looked like a little pint-sized me in the fancy matching clothes sets they bought him. I'm not cheap, but they were too generous to give me time to buy my son clothes. But, then, I don't like shopping anyway and would be just as appreciative if Mom and Sheila bought my clothes while they were shopping for Ray-Ray.

I don't remember my father going into a store to shop, ever. How did he get his clothes? Mom must have shopped for him like she was shopping for Ray-Ray. It always seemed unreal that my father was never coming home again. Death disturbs our expected flow of events. But, he wasn't coming. He hadn't been since the day the undertaker took his body out. Mom told us his heart had given out. I remember thinking why did it give out? Was there nothing more it had to give? Why do some hearts keep going whether anything is being given or not, and some hearts stop? Why did my father die?

At the park next to the river, Ray-Ray picked up more stones than he could throw. I could figure out his thinking, even at his age. In his three-year-old mind he knew if he stuffed his pockets with shiny white and gray stones, he wouldn't have to come back up the bank to the parking area to get stones to chunk into the river. He already knew that there were no stones down near the water, nothing but dark, black dirt like rich chocolate brownies. The mind of a three-year-old was now my most interesting life puzzle.

"Chunk it hard, Ray-Ray," I said. I threw one of my stones sideways so it would skim across the water like a flickering, dancing light as it seared the top of the river surface. I counted five hits on the surface. That had been a fun trick every since I was a boy, skimming the water surface with my stone thrown sideways. I don't remember my father ever bringing my brothers and me to the river to throw stones. Maybe he was too busy doing grown-up stuff. Wasn't I grown? Didn't I have the sense to share in my three-year-old son's play? It was a joy that couldn't be bought.

The Savannah River was not a restless river. It seemed content to meander from South Carolina down past Savannah and out to the Atlantic. It made its way slowly out to the ocean, zigzagging around curves and past houses as simple as shacks and as elaborate as the homes in the gated communities that kept the rich, mostly white, from the average income folks along the way. What the river must have felt when sucked into the tumult of the bustling Atlantic at the end of its journey was a mystery. When the fresh water meets the salty water of the sea, I imagine the ocean is in command.

Ray-Ray was tossing his stones rapidly onto the surface of the water. The stones were free. The time we were having together could not be purchased. I knew Angela would have stood with us, and tossed stones out on the river. She and I had tossed stones in the river as young lovers when I first learned to drive and brought her down to this same riverbank for kissing under the open sky.

The sea gulls did aero pirouettes upside down, diving towards faint moving shadows in the Port-colored waters, and flying skyward again with their afternoon meal, fish in their beaks. Over and over, these airborne kamikaze acrobats displayed their skills like the celebrated Air Force Thunderbirds air shows. Nature had tricks older than metal and machinery. I watched intensely. Then, a shadow of a feeling descended over me. I turned quickly to where Ray-Ray was standing beside me. That second seemed like a lifetime. I felt this sense of utter and impossible loss. Ray-Ray had slipped into a hole in the river bank. I stooped, reached down into the dark, moist hole and grabbed for him. I caught the back of his shirt. I pulled him up out of the ground in one swoop. I held him tight to my chest, black mud covering his torso and squishing in my hand. I breathed in the dirt, the air, the evening. Ray-Ray looked up at me as though he was the prize in a real fun game. Despite my sense of danger and possible loss, I smiled back at him and squeezed him close. Even the bank of the river, which offered life, could take life. The river is strange work, life-giving, and life-taking, magnificent and treacherous.

Ray-Ray and I rode back into Savannah in silence. He looked ready for a nap. I felt I must stay awake forever to ensure his safety. I thought about my father's silence. I knew then that I could never penetrate it. Sheila said he was a drunk. Was he a drunk because of the silence? Was he a drunk because of me? Had his family moved him away from a sober course? Or, was there something else in his past that made him seek solitude in drinking? And, did the drinking keep him from sharing his words and arms openly with his sons and daughter and wife. Or was it the family, his wife, the pressures of raising a family in the times in which we lived that removed him from us? Some questions have no answers and though they may be asked, I did no longer feel cheated by his silence. I had all I could do to raise my son in the time that I would have. I knew what I must do to bring the quest to uncover a man who was me from the mystery that was him.

The next afternoon I left Ray-Ray with the teenager next door who had become my main babysitter. He and Ray-Ray fed off each other's affection and when they got together I was lost to them as they played games of escape from adult tyranny.

"Mom, I think I owe you an apology," I said.

"You always owe me something, Big Man, so if it's gonna cost me, keep it."

Was she still upset with me? In my whole life we had never had a moment of disagreement, even when she had to take a belt to my backside for some devilment.

"Mom, are you mad at me?" I asked.

"Big Man, I worship the ground you walk on. I'm your momma, I can't be mad at my child. Now, if you and Ray-Ray don't come over for Sunday's dinner, then I don't know. I might change." She laughed.

I took Mom in my arms and gave her a big hug. She was tough, but she was easy.

I stopped by Sheila's house later. Her husband and I had a beer. He seemed to relish my company, having someone to have a beer with. Then Sheila got home from work. I found a moment alone with her.

"Sheila, I'm sorry for not listening to you the other day. Sorry for being so cantankerous, my darling sister."

That's a big word, Big Man. 'Cantankerous.' And it's big of you to be trying to offer an apology." She smiled at me just like Mom always did.

"I ain't apologizing, I'm just saying I'm sorry," I said.

"Whatever, Big Man, have your way." She was both serious and kidding.

"Okay, then don't try to feed me. Mom stuffed me, okay?"

On the drive home, I was thankful for the women in my life, thankful for my father, silent but responsible, for working everyday of our lives to feed us. I was thankful for the River of Heaven, its many wonders and mysteries. I promised myself to be visible and present to Ray-Ray, and try to answer questions for him.

-11-

ROLLBACK

"God changes things." Reverend Howell was getting ready for his whoop. His voice became deeper and he straddled the pulpit like a seaman at the helm in a coming storm.

"Wanna go home, Daddy." Ray-Ray had been quietly and attentively darting his eyes back and forth during the service. I watched him follow the choir with participatory joy, bobbing his head and lifting his feet, which dangled from the pew, in response to the rhythms of the singing. He was right on beat with the drummer. He looked mesmerized. I smiled. He was easy in public. I felt people were often looking at me asking, "Does he think he can raise that boy all by himself?"

"That your little man?" or "That your big boy?" Frequent questions from the ladies I'd run into who quickly did the eye dart to my ring finger.

"And, where is your mommy?" or something like that they'd ask as a follow-up to make certain I was single. Then I'd get the pity like my wife had left me or maybe I was just a no-good "baby daddy."

Ray-Ray gave me lots of benefits when he was tagging along beside me. Ladies loved the little three-year-old with the curly brown hair. And every time they rubbed his head, they licked their lips at me. I wasn't mad with Ray-Ray at all. I got more attention with him from eligible females, though I had never been a slouch in the ladies department.

I usually accommodated my son. Not indulgently but practically. He had lost his mother, who had given him into my care just before her death. But we were strangers then. Now I had to take responsibility as a father and a parent. I couldn't just get up and walk out of church just when the preacher was about to bring Heaven home.

"I'll give you a dollar to be quiet 'til the preacher stops preaching. Okay, Ray-Ray?" I said.

Ray-Ray high-fived me right as the preacher went into a whoop.

I could see Mom and Sheila in the same pew down front that they had always sat in. Wasn't surprised that Sheila's husband wasn't there. My father never came to church with us either. There wasn't even a question about it. It was like church was outside of something he did. In Savannah, which is the heart of the Bible Belt, there is a church on every corner and a storefront church in the middle of every strip mall, but the churchgoers are predominately female, old, young and children. My father didn't belong in church, but my mother paid his tithes for him every Sunday. It was like an insurance policy and it paid off in the end because my father's funeral was held in the church like he was a bonafide member. Only other times I recall him being in church were when he walked my sister Sheila down the aisle at her wedding, at my wedding, and when Mom had him renew their wedding vows. He did not look uncomfortable either time. One thing I recall about my father is that he always looked like he was comfortable and everybody else was out of place.

The pastor segued into "The Old Ship of Zion," as he came out of his sermon, and the choir began singing on cue with him.

Ray-Ray began to twist and turn and kick out his feet from his pew seat. I took his hand and squeezed it gently to reassure him I had not forgotten my promise.

"Is there anyone here that needs to get his soul out of the lost and found? Come on down," called the pastor, ending his spirited invitational to join the church.

I didn't see it coming. In a bounce, Ray-Ray was out of his seat and on his way to the front of the church.

"Ray-Ray," I called. It was too late.

The pastor smiled at Ray-Ray. I didn't know what to expect. The secretary of the church took her place beside the pastor to get the name of whoever might join the church.

"Who's with this young man?" the pastor asked.

I stood up.

"Please come and stand beside him." the pastor asked.

I walked down to the front of the church and stood behind the chair where Ray-Ray sat calmly.

The congregation became very quiet. I felt like all eyes were on me. I didn't turn around to see what expressions were on Mom and Sheila's face. I was thinking I've shown I don't have control of my three-year-old now.

"Thank you, Brother Johnson, for coming to stand by this handsome child." The pastor spoke so the congregation could hear him. Then he leaned to me and said, "He's too young to make this decision of faith direction, but we can baptize him with your consent."

Then pastor spoke to Ray-Ray. "What do you want, my young brother?"

Quicker than spit, Ray-Ray answered.

"I wanna go home." Laughter sprang from the congregation. I joined them hesitantly.

"Very well," said the pastor. "Say 'amen,' church." There was a chorus of Amens that filled the church.

"Now, repeat after me." He raised his right hand in the air. "May the Lord watch over me and thee while we are absent one from another. Amen." Again, the church bellowed forth Amens.

In the parking lot outside of the church, I moved quickly towards my car, Ray-Ray in tow.

"Big Man," It was Mom. I hadn't moved fast enough. I turned and went to the place where she stood. I had been summoned.

"I know, Mom. I don't know what got into Ray-Ray."

"I know what got into him," Mom had a glint in her eye. "He just walked down the aisle. He was too fast for me to stop him."

"His daddy probably got into him," Mom said. "Sheila, you remember that time I took y'all to the Holy Roller church, and the preacher was preaching and he asked, 'Who in here needs some money?' Remember that? Do you remember, Big Man?" She nodded at me and went on looking in Sheila's direction.

"I remember." My sister looked like a conspirator.

"Yep, Big Man got up and raised his hand. Even the preacher was taken aback. He hadn't expected anybody to answer. What happened then, Big Man?"

"I don't remember," I said.

"He gave you a ten dollar bill. And you were mighty happy. You acted like you had struck gold. Remember, Sheila?"

"I remember," Sheila said. "I'd say Ray-Ray is just like his father."

Ray-Ray had only been on the planet for three years, but in those three years he had developed a mystery of his own. Sometimes he'd do things and I wouldn't know where they came from. He wasn't an "old people's child" as they said, because Angela and I were in our early thirties when he was born.

Ray-Ray stood next to me in the bathroom as I was shaving. He was pretending that he was shaving, too.

"Ain't no sunshine when she gone," he sang out.

I stopped shaving and looked down at him.

"Where did you learn that song, Ray-Ray?" I asked. It was one of my favorite songs but I didn't recall singing it in the short time Ray-Ray had been living with me.

"Ah house is not ah home. Ah house is not ah home." He sang it twice.

"Where did you learn that song, Ray-Ray?" I asked again.

"Diamond," he said.

"Diamond? Who's Diamond?"

"Ah house is not ah home anytime she goes away," he sang.

"Who's Diamond, Ray-Ray? Is she a singer?"

"No."

"Did you hear her on TV?"

"No. Ain't no sunshine when she's gone." He sang the "no" louder than before, like a blues singer.

"Where does Diamond sing, Ray-Ray?"

"She a bird."

"Where did you learn that song?"

"Diamond." He stopped pretending he was shaving and went out into the hall and picked up the basketball my mother had given him.

Ray-Ray would surprise me with the things he'd say and sometimes by the way he acted. We were at Sheila's one afternoon and her dog, Puddles, came in the house. Sheila didn't like Puddles in the house.

"Get outta here with your stinky self," Sheila said to Puddles. Ray-Ray went over to Puddles and patted her and said, "Roll over." Puddles laid on the carpet and rolled over. I watched curiously. How did Ray-Ray know to tell Puddles to roll over?

The plane was flying over the gray conglomerate of bleak commercial warehouse and industrial buildings that make up part the Newark landscape as it made our descent into Newark Liberty International Airport. It was faster to get to New York City from Newark's airport than from LaGuardia or JFK, and cheaper. Angela's mother had asked me to go to Brooklyn to square away some unsettled business for my deceased ex-wife. In a way I was the best choice for the task. Angela and I had lived together in New York for almost ten years when we were married. I knew the city, Angela's mother did not. Besides, she seemed overwrought with all the discoveries pouring out of Angela's life. There really wasn't much to do. Close up Angela's apartment, check on any valuables she had, and plan to have her furniture sold. Her landlord had been very cooperative over the phone and Angela's mom had given me specific instructions and power of attorney.

I turned the key to Angela's apartment. My eyes blurred up on me. Maybe I had some eerie notion that Angela would be there, face all bright, gorgeous and ready to take me in her arms. The apartment was dark, gray and a gloom had settled there like it was waiting to be released.

I stretched out on Angela's bed and flicked on the TV with the remote control near the bed. The last time I had been in this room, my ex-wife was alive. We had even planned to spend a night of love-making in this room, in this bed. Now there were whispers and shadows and words not said, and thoughts floating in ether about my head. I was not alone. Angela was still in my heart.

I called Sheila so I could say goodnight to Ray-Ray.

"Hey, sis."

"Everything okay, Big Man? You have a good flight?"

"Yes, sis. Ray-Ray still up?"

"Here he is, Big Man. He's got his PJ's on, ready for bed."

"Hi, Ray-Ray," I said. It was strange hearing his small voice coming through the grayness of his mother's apartment. It was so clear it seemed to run the shadows out of the bedroom.

"Where are you, Daddy? You comin' to get me?"

"I'm coming to get you real soon, Ray-Ray. You be a big boy, okay?"

"Okay. Can I come with you?"

"No. I'm coming back to you. You be good, okay?"

"I'm going to bed. I'm sleepy. I have my red Spidaman pajamas on that Aunt Sheila bought me. Do you like them?"

"Yeah, I like them, Ray-Ray. I love my boy, okay?"

"Okay."

"Now let me speak to Aunt Sheila."

Ray-Ray said goodbye and Sheila came on the phone. I felt like a man stranded in an unsettled space. I was in the apartment of the woman I had once promised to spend my whole life with and now she was gone from me forever, and I'd been listening to the voice of a son she bore me, kept from me, and now he was comforting his father. I had a feeling something unexpected was coming my way.

The ringing of Angela's apartment doorbell was like an alarm going off. I had not slept well all night and dozed off around 6 a.m. into a deep sleep. Now I was being summoned by a doorbell.

I slipped into my pants and went to the door.

"You're Gary, Big Man," the pretty woman at the door said. "I'm Carla, Angela's friend. Her mom said you would be coming and asked me to give you some things. I've got an appointment with a publisher now and won't be back until this evening so I brought some things by to get you started. I know it must be hard and all. Well, let me slow down and give you what I got."

"Okay," I said. Her eyes were bright and wide open, with a lively twinkle. She had fair skin with ample breasts under her smart white silk blouse. She was slender and curvy and about as tall as Angela. She seemed full of life, pretty, and there was a freshness about her that was like washed clothes on an open line. The shadows disappeared in Angela's apartment.

"What was your name again?" I asked.

"I'm Carla. I live in the apartment two doors down. Angela's mom called me. Sorry I couldn't make it to Angela's funeral. Really sorry about that but I know Angela would have understood. She always understood what I was up to, and what was going on with me. Well, before I get to running off at the mouth again, I'll check on you around six, if you want me to. I'll ring the bell, okay? If you want to answer, okay. If not I'll go on back to my place. You look just like Angela described you, and just like your pictures. What else? Oh, I'm gone. Wait, Here is my cell number if you need … Bye."

She turned from me and walked away. She possessed the low key-glamorousness and confidence of Jada Pinkett and seductive moves of a Halle Berry. I hadn't been able to get a word in. She was a lively woman. She reminded me of somebody but I couldn't put in my mind who.

I knew I was supposed to meet this woman that Angela knew in her apartment building, but I imagined she was going to be an old woman.

Carla rang Angela's apartment bell at exactly six o'clock.

"Here is Angela's safe deposit key duplicate and the combination to her P. O. box. We sometimes picked up each other's mail. And here is a coat I got from her last winter and forgot to return," she said.

"You can keep the coat," I said. "I'm sure Angela would want you to have it."

"It was one of her favorites, you know," she said.

"Yes, I know. I bought it for her."

"Oh, I'm sorry," she said.

"It's all right," I said. "We were divorced for a few years."

"Not to hear her tell it. She said you would always be her man. Do you mind if I call you Big Man? That's what Angela always called you."

By seven we were having dinner at the Thai restaurant across the street from the apartment building. I was grateful for her help and needed company, so I had invited her to join me. She was a talker, so I did not have to worry about feeling alone.

"How is Ray-Ray? I kinda didn't want to ask because I miss him so much. You know you don't want to mention people you know you will miss as soon as their names come out of your mouth but then your mind has already begun to miss them for you. You know what I mean?"

"No. I don't know what you mean," I said.

"Yes, you do. You just don't want to think about it or to indulge me, one or the other."

Even her way of talking and thinking felt comfortable to me.

"You mean like you want to think about them but you don't want to think about them, and not wanting to think about them, you think about them all the more. Something convoluted like that."

"Precisely. See. You know. Ray-Ray used to have so much fun playing with my dog, Ransom, and Ransom loved Ray-Ray. Ransom would roll over and sit up, and bark, or whatever Ray-Ray wanted him to do. Ray-Ray learns fast."

I smiled. First time I had smiled since I left Savannah. It felt good.

During dinner I learned that she had been a screenwriter in L.A. and had some success there. She was in a project turning one of Angela's stories to film but it didn't work out. Angela had suggested she move back to New York. She did. She had stayed with Angela until she got the apartment two doors down.

"I went with her to the hospital when Ray-Ray was born. I hated you then, you know?"

"Really. I hadn't done anything. I didn't even know you."

"Yeah. I wondered what kind of man you were. I asked Angela, 'What kind of man could be the father of his child and not be here when he's born? Then, she explained everything.'"

"What did she say?" Seemed like I could hear Angela over my shoulder saying, "See, Big Man, you want to know every detail."

"She explained that you were a good man. That she really didn't deserve you. She said, 'He is like water. True.' I liked that."

"What did she mean?"

"She told me she had not been the easiest wife. That she had been with you since you were kids and she wanted to get away and see if she had – how did she put it? – 'mind legs.' She wanted to see if she could think for herself, be something on her own. That she didn't want to leave you but you couldn't sorta see who she was in your shadow. But she got pregnant. You always had the answers, she said. I understood that. That was the same reason I left Savannah and moved to New York. My daddy had a long, thick shadow and I couldn't see me in it."

I wanted to kiss her. I wanted to move around the table and take her in my arms and kiss her. I wanted to touch her and hold her. I sat there and let her fill my eyes.

She looked at her watch. "I've got to go. It's nine o'clock. I've got to feed Diamond," she said.

"Diamond. Who's Diamond?"

"Diamond's my parrot. I always feed Diamond at nine. Without fail. My cell phone alarm will be going off in a minute. Can we leave? I hate to rush you."

"You don't mind rushing me. I got a feeling you don't mind doing whatever you want to do, Carla," I said.

"Why is that?" she asked.

"Because you seem to do just what you want." I said.

"Mostly. That's another reason I had to get away from home. I didn't want my daddy telling me what to do. He's a smart man, but I wanted to see if I could be smart on my own. Let's go, okay?"

I knew now who Carla reminded me of.

We said goodnight to each other when we got off the elevator.

"Thanks for the dinner. Maybe tomorrow you can come to my apartment for dinner, okay?"

"Okay," I said. She turned around when she got to her door.

"Say seven-thirty. It's here." She opened her apartment door and was gone into another world that I could not see. She reminded me of my mother. Sure. Quick on the uptake. Just gracious and kind enough to make you think she needed your help.

"Ain't no sunshine when she's gone. Ain't no sunshine when she's gone." Diamond looked like she was wearing an old coat. Most of her feathers looked like they were on their last days.

"How old is Diamond?" I asked.

"A house just ain't no home," Diamond sang in a rich parrot contralto.

"In parrot years, Diamond is seventy-five years old."

"How many years is that in human years?"

"In human years, that's seventy-five years old."

"You could be a real smart aleck, I bet," I said.

"You could be right. No. Diamond was my grandmother's parrot. Had been with her until she died at ninety. Nobody really liked Diamond but me. It's the one song, do you think? Anyway, I loved Diamond since I was a kid. I told my father I would take her when Grammy died. He acted like that was too much of a burden on me but I think he was glad Diamond was moving on. Diamond used to drink gin with Grammy and the two of them used to cuss. I used to snigger at it. My mom and dad were not too happy to have cussing around their churchgoing household, but I thought it was a sign of freedom. I helped Diamond escape and she seems to thrive on being her own woman. Grammy used to also smoke a pipe and blow smoke rings at Diamond when they got tipsy on gin. And, the two of them would cuss. I liberated Diamond from Dad and Mom."

"Damn right. You damn right. Ain't no sunshine when she's gone." Diamond's contralto fired up again.

"You and Angela's must have been very close friends."

'The closest. I took care of Ray-Ray during the day because I was home writing while Angela was working in the editorial department. We alternated fixing dinner. I was the better cook though Angela could throw down from time to time. But, I got her off all those fried Savannah make-you-die-quick fattening meals. We laughed together. We cried together. After y'all got divorced, she even stayed over some nights. I was the one that used to tell her, 'Girl, call that man and go on over there and get you some. Lest you know what you getting.'"

I looked away, over at Diamond.

"Ain't no sunshine. Ain't no sunshine." Diamond sounded like she was ready for sleep.

'You really liked Angela. She was special." I said.

"Yeah. There was Angela and there was Angela. If you know what I mean. She wasn't always easy. But then who is?"

It didn't take me long to finish up Angela's business. Everyone was cooperative. The landlord was even going to help me have a street sale. I let her take some of the furniture for herself. I didn't want anything. I did decide to stay in New York for a week. I needed the time. Sheila said Ray-Ray was fine and I shouldn't worry.

I had almost forgotten about the incident that had made me pack up and leave New York until I decided to call some of the old Savannah neighborhood crowd living in New York. Almost every one of the people I called reminded me of the incident. Apparently, it had become something like folklore among the group. I had to keep straightening them out about the details. One person said I had cut off everybody's coat in the coat closet at a Halloween party to get even with BeeBee and Cynthia for cutting off my coat sleeves. Another person said I had a coat fetish or something and had to see a shrink to get over it. Each time, I told it like it was. BeeBee had borrowed my best blue suit for his son for a funeral. The demonic numb skull was a half a head shorter than me and BeeBee and Cynthia had cut off the pants legs and I did not find out until I got the suit back. I only cut off BeeBee and Cynthia's coat sleeves at a Christmas party in retaliation, for which they had me put in jail. It did sound weird when I was trying to straighten the story out. I decided I would never mention it again, and if it came up in my presence, I'd change the subject, period. I could do that in a heartbeat.

I saw Carla every day for the week I was in New York. On the last evening, I took her for dinner at the Thai restaurant across from the apartment building. I had a feeling. My spine started tingling.

I could hear my father speaking to me as I sat at the table looking at Carla, with the traffic, lights and moving people as a backdrop in the large window behind her.

"What you gon do with that woman, boy?" I heard my father. He was standing right behind my chair. I didn't mind. I had a bold surprise for him.

"How do you like the wine, Big Man?" Carla smiled.

"Carla, will you marry me?" I said it clear and like it was the right thing at the right time.

"Do you love me, Big Man?"

"Yes. I do. I sure enough do." My voice rang clear and strong again.

"Maybe I will, Big Man. Let's give it some time, okay?"

It was done.

-12-

NAKED

Sometimes we do things despite ourselves, things that we could not imagine ourselves doing.

Two months had passed since I met Carla.

"Would you be the best man at my wedding?" I had asked the question. It was dead silent on the other end. I could hear nothing, not even breathing.

"Did we lose the connection? Did you hear me?" I asked.

"Yeah. I heard you. I heard you, right. Yes. I dunno what to say, man. Damn straight. If you want me."

"Yes. I want you. I'll give you all the 411 later. Just starting to line up my part. It's gonna be in two weeks."

"Two weeks. Wow. That's fast. Do I know the lucky sister?"

"No. I don't think so. She from New York."

"A New York momma, huh? Well, bless your bones. You gon come on over to the lock up, brother."

"'Bout time, don't you think?"

"Whatever you need, let me know. I can talk about it right?"

"Yeah, BeeBee. My mom and Sheila will be broadcasting it all over Savannah before sundown. I just told them."

"Text me day, time, place, etc. I'm gonna clear life space for this one. That's what's up. You gonna get with me about tux rental and all that, right? It is gonna be traditional, huh? You know you're known for doing your own thing? I can't get over it man."

"She's a traditional kind of woman, so yes, but we will be moving fast," I said.

Carla's mother and father were deceased, both died last year, and she was an only child, military tumbleweed with no tie-down roots. She was fine with having her wedding in Savannah. She said she only planned to invite two close girlfriends. Sheila had agreed to be the wedding planner, which meant Mom would be looking over her shoulder every inch of the way. All Carla and I had to do was show up for rehearsal and then get married.

"Ray-Ray, do you remember Ms. Carla?"

"Carla. Uh huh."

"And Diamond?"

Ray-Ray drew his lips in and his head back, "Ain't no sunshine when she's gone."

"That's right, Ray-Ray. Carla is going to marry me, okay?"

"Okay."

I don't know if he understood, but I had to tell him.

"So, Carla will be coming to live with us." I said.

"Diamond is coming to live with us?"

"Do you want Diamond to come to live with us?"

"Can sing with Diamond?"

"Yes, you can sing with Diamond."

"Can Diamond sleep in my room?"

"We will see, okay?"

That was easier than I thought. I still don't know what goes on in Ray-Ray's head.

Sheila and Mom were in their element. They had talked with Carla over the phone more than a few times since I broke the news to them.

"I really like her." Mom said. "What does she look like? I'm sure she's pretty. Carla is a pretty name." She had called me in between calling Carla and Sheila.

"I thought you would, Mom."

"Does she go to church?"

"Yes."

"What faith? Oh, never mind that. They are all the same long as they got one God."

"Yes, she is pretty. And don't you go trying to fatten her up when she gets here."

"She's skinny?"

"No, Mom. She's your size. You want to know something else?"

"What's that? Don't tell me nothing strange 'cause I've already taken a liking to Carla. I hope she's not a weightlifter or in one of them strange religious cults.

"Mom, she looks a lot like you. Just lighter. And she's not in a cult."

"You only just met this woman. I don't mind helping Sheila plan the wedding and everything, but this is kind of fast, isn't it?"

"When it's right, why be slow?"

"You got a point there, Big Man. That's the way it was with me and your father. I just don't want you to get hurt. And you've got Ray-Ray to think of now."

"Mom, I told you, Carla was Angela's best friend in New York. She kept Ray-Ray every day while Angela was working."

"We're so happy Big Man, but if she does anything wrong to you, I'll put a foot on her like squashing an ant."

"Whoa, Mom, I'm not a baby."

"You my baby. You will always be, diaper or no diaper, you hear?"

I knew Mom would like Carla because Carla told Sheila that she wasn't much on planning and fancy stuff. She would get her gown and leave everything else up to her. She wired Sheila a bank draft for the cost of everything. According to Sheila, Carla was going to have money in the bank because the bank note was twice what she needed to have an absolutely splendid wedding.

"That was too funny when your son came down during the invitation, Brother Johnson. I actually thought he was trying to join the church," Pastor Miller said.

"Yes, pastor. He caught me off guard, too."

"Brother Johnson, your future wife called me. Then, of course, your sister called, and your dear mother has called three times in the last two days. As far as the church is concerned, that is, as far as I am concerned, everything is a go for your wedding. The chairman of the Trustee Board approved the use of the space and the church had nothing else on its calendar that Saturday."

"That's good," I said.

"But ..." he said.

I didn't like 'But.'

"What is it?"

"Usually the bride requests the church, and if she's a member and the time is available, it's okay. Church always gets a donation."

"We are going to give the church a donation. My sister Sheila will take care of it."

"It's not that. Your wife is not a member of the church."

"I know. But, I am."

"No, Brother Johnson, you're not. And even that wouldn't matter if it wasn't for this other thing."

"I was baptized in this church. I almost said I was born in this church. "I've been in this church my whole life. My mother and family have sat on that same pew since she first came to this church as a baby with her mother, who sat on that same pew for three generations."

"That might be true. I've only been here for ten years. But your name is not on the roll. Every few years the church purges the roll."

I was getting flustered now. "I've been going to this church ever since I returned to Savannah. You've seen me in this church every Sunday. I pay my tithes. Now, it's me and my son."

"Well the church clerk checked the roster and you never rejoined the church after you left and came back."

"Why did the church clerk do that? I've always been a member of this church. My great-grandfather laid that cornerstone on the front of this church my daddy told me."

"That might be. I'm not disputing your word, Brother Johnson. I'm caught in a hard place here. I got to follow the rules. Sister Donna Nolan, the church clerk, raised this issue in board meeting last night and she made some good points."

I felt the blood rush to my head. I could see the palms of my hands turn red. Donna, Angela's half sister, she was the church clerk. We had dated, even been serious. I had wanted to marry her, not knowing she was the half sister of my ex-wife. I had wanted her to have my children. Sometimes we don't even know when God steps in to stop us from tragedy. Here she was again, wreaking havoc with my life. I didn't even try to figure it out. Donna's own sister, my ex, had said Donna was crazy.

"So what am I supposed to do, Pastor?"

"I can call around for you to see if there is another church available, two Saturday's from now, is it?"

I wanted to bust his lip, but I thought he'd just have a busted lip and I'd look like a fool. I got up from the seat in his office and extended my hand.

"Thank you, Pastor. I'll get back to you." I'd come at his request. I thought the meeting was to involve pastor counseling for Carla and me, and to get his commitment to performing the service. I left calmly.

"I would have jacked him up," BeeBee said. I could picture BeeBee with his construction worker hands holding the pastor up in the air.

"Nah. Something'll work out. I just saw your car outside the barbershop on my way past and though I'd stop and tell you about the tux bit. Lloyd, Reggie Clark and my cousin Skip will be the groomsmen. So we can all go together for the fitting."

"Only thing I want to do right now is fit my size twelve in the preacher's holy of holies."

I decided to go right to the serpent. I called Donna.

"Donna, what's going on? The pastor tells me you object to my fiancé and me using our family church to get married."

"Hi, Big Man. It's good to hear your voice."

"Oh, come off it Donna. Why are you doing this?"

"I'm not doing anything, Big Man."

"You know exactly what you're doing. I've been at that church all my life."

"So. My family been there, too. You not the only one."

"Is it because it didn't work out between us, Donna?"

"What was it that you wanted to work out? You wanted me to have some stupid children so you could drive them crazy. No, sir, it didn't work out."

"What do you want, Donna?"

"I want my sister back. You took a long time out of her life. Now she's in a grave and you want to take a strange woman and have her raise Angela's son. I can't stop you, but the Lord will see to it that you don't have any luck, I promise you. I'm down on my knees praying for it."

I was hearing demons.

"Well, you better get up off your knees before you have the calluses of Hell. You messed up my life once. I was the crazy one. But, not again. I got it now. Angela said once that you wanted everything that she had. Now you want everything that Angela could have had. But, it won't work, Donna." I hung up. It was hard to catch my breath.

I decided to go down to the high school and shoot some hoops on the school yard to clear my heat and to stop my heart from pumping like a massive oil rigger.

After an hour at the school basketball court, I put my ball in my car and headed home. As I passed the church I saw the pastor's and Donna's cars parked there. I pulled into the rear parking lot of the church, got out of my car and started walking around the side of the church. When I got to the window near the pastor's study, I stopped, hearing mumbling voices coming from within.

"That's what he said." It was the pastor speaking.

"Well, good for him." It was Donna.

"You know I'd do anything for you, baby."

"I know that." Donna was speaking.

Then it became quieter. There were muffled sounds and rustling clothes and things being moved about. I heard it all. Twenty minutes later, I waited outside the side door to the parking lot where their cars were parked.

Donna came out first. Her mouth fell wide open when she saw me standing there. She looked like she was about to be strangled. She glanced back at the church door, thought better of it, let out a gasp and hauled tail to her car and drove off.

In a few minutes, the pastor came out. He had a smug, satisfied grin on his face. He didn't see me as close as I was to the door. I spoke.

"You know you're wrong," I said. His eyes shot up in his head. In a second I grabbed him, penned his head to the brick wall and breathed fire in his face. Teeth clenched, I made every syllable I spoke have its own place in the universe.

"You will be at the church Saturday after next. You will perform my wedding ceremony. You will rehearse with me and my fiancé and the wedding party the Friday before. And you will have a smile on your face to light up Calvary. Do you understand?" I ground the back of his head into the red brick wall to emphasize my seriousness. When I let him go, he smiled at me.

I was nervous as the wedding party started falling in place. I kept letting my mind get beyond our wedding day so I could take the pressure off myself. I kept thinking about playing basketball with Ray-Ray, and my new wife sitting on the sidelines cheering her men on. I thought of my father. I could see him as a young man, showing me as a boy how to make a layup. I could see that smile on his face every time I made my shot. He knew I was going to be a good basketball player, I could tell it, even then. I worked hard at the game, concentrating to be good so I could please him.

Lloyd looked like he stepped out a high fashion magazine. He was still checking himself out in his tux. Lloyd's white, white teeth made stood out against the dark blue tuxedo. The arms of his tux bulged with his ripping muscles. His reddish-purple lips held their own in that strong face, accentuated by his thick, bushy, black-as-midnight upward curving eyebrows. My cousin, Skip, was comfortably at ease in his tux and busy texting somebody on his cell. Scooter had been visiting with me for two days prior to the wedding. He and Ray-Ray had hit it off immediately. He was eighteen now, and his strong mustache gave him a look of a man. His tux fitted perfectly, not like Lloyd's but like an unassuming, young man wholly at peace with himself and still anxious for what the world had to offer.

"You need anything, Big Man? Some water? Nervous? You don't look nervous. You look cool," Scooter was always helpful. I'm glad we'd kept the relationship going. I had promised him last night I'd come to his college in the fall for his first basketball game. I liked thinking that I had passed on some skills to him. Meanwhile he had a summer job as a tour guide at the Arizona State Museum. He said they told him he could have the job every summer while in college. He had passed the tour guide test with a perfect score.

"Yeah, I'm nervous. I'm just hiding it real good. This is like saying goodbye to my feet. I might never be able to walk again after today." Scooter punched me on the shoulder playfully.

Scooter had brought me news from Tucson. Seems Bobby, my old housekeeper had become a minister and opened a church of her own. Half the folks from our old church followed her and her ministry was growing like anything. Bobby had found her calling or it had found her. As they say 'To whom much is given, much is required.' All I could think was 'Rock on, Bobby.' If anybody could clean up unclean souls it would be Bobby.

BeeBee, my best man, was the last to come. I saw him get out of his car through the church window where I was preoccupied with not being preoccupied. I saw BeeBee kiss Cynthia as she let him off in the filled, small church parking lot. Cynthia was all spruced up in a bright yellow dress. She looked pretty, even. BeeBee was running late as usual. He was still working two jobs and falling behind in doing whatever he was supposed to be doing. All of the guys went to the tuxedo fitting together but BeeBee had to have me pick up his tux for him. He couldn't even find time to pick up his tux in his double-duty job schedule.

"Hey, man, you are late." I grinned at BeeBee. He was perspiring more than me. "And, you look nervous."

BeeBee said, "You ain't married yet so how could I be late?"

Lloyd said, "You are all out of breath, BeeBee. You had better knock off some of that chicken eatin' and get on the court more, my man."

"You aren't married yet, Big Man, so I'm not late. Long as you get to the wedding before the bride, who's always late, you're on time. Where's my tux man?" BeeBee said.

"You couldn't even pick up your own tux. That's sorry, man. I bet you've got grease under those fingernails, too," Lloyd said.

"Where's my tux, Big Man? I don't have time to be harassed by a metrosexual, manicured, mannequin like Lloyd," BeeBee said.

"Whoa, brothers, it's my wedding day," I threw my hands up in the air.

"Lloyd, we can take this to the basketball court another day, unless you have to get your nails done, bro," BeeBee said.

I handed BeeBee the black tuxedo bag.

"Court? You better stop courting yourself. I hear Cynthia's pregnant. After all this time and Jonathan is almost grown, man. You just couldn't control yourself, huh?"

BeeBee took the tux bag and began to unzip it. He said, "Lloyd, I got your control, right here, deep in my right pocket."

We all laughed. But BeeBee was sweating more now.

"Hey, bro, it's my wedding day. Slow down, enjoy the ride," I said.

"Put on the dang tuxedo, man. You scared to take off your clothes in front of the guys?" Lloyd asked.

BeeBee striped down fast. His red, white and blue boxer shorts light up the place.

"Real American," said my cousin Skip.

Everybody laughed.

BeeBee pulled the tux from the bag and started to put his right leg in the tux pants.

"What the sand gnats!" he exclaimed.

Everybody stared at him in disbelief. Laughter broke out.

The tux pant leg was a foot too short.

"What is this?" BeeBee dark complexion turned red.

"Payback, Mac," I said.

"That's funny, man." Lloyd looked beside himself.

"That's crazy," said my cousin. "What's that about?"

I reached in the chair beside me and handed BeeBee a pair of tuxedo pants.

"Here's the real ones, BeeBee. Just jerking your chain. Those are some old tux pants I bought at Good Will."

"Why'd you do that?" Skip asked.

"It's a long, old story. Once BeeBee had a pair of my best suit pants cut off."

"That's not funny, Big Man," BeeBee said.

Lloyd patted me on the back.

"I didn't think so either," I said

My mother stuck her head in the door.

The guys let out a chorus of "Mrs. Johnsons."

"What're you men doing? The bride's car is pulling up. Get in here." Mom smiled like a Beauty Queen contestant, then politely closed the door.

BeeBee and the boys looked handsome in our matching tuxedos. Even better than in our old school basketball uniforms. And Ray-Ray was the most self-confident ring bearer this side of the Mississippi.

Carla looked even prettier on our wedding day than I could have imagined. I could hear my father whisper in my ear as she came down the aisle, "Here she is."

I had my wife, my son, my family and friends around me.

ABOUT THE AUTHOR

Ja A. Jahannes is a novelist, essayist, playwright, poet and composer. His work has been published in numerous anthologies. He has had twelve plays produced in regional theater, and two operas produced nationally. He is a frequent columnist for several publications and a contributing editor for two international online magazines.

www.ingramcontent.com/pod-product-compliance
Lightning Source LLC
Chambersburg PA
CBHW060122260626
47160CB00005B/1981